FUNNY BUSINESS

THE BRODIE BROTHERS SERIES

KAYLEY LORING

PROLOGUE - OWEN

Three-ish Years Ago

It's about five minutes before I'm supposed to take the stage, and my phone vibrates in my pocket. After four years of marriage, I know it's my wife before I even check the Caller ID. She's always had a knack for calling at a bad time, but I can't decline it—not with the way things have been going since we got to her parents' house. That would be like giving her entire family a hammer to drive that final disappointed nail into my coffin. I head back toward the club's kitchen before answering.

"Hey, what's up? I have to go on in five minutes."

The loud exhale is her standard greeting for me these days. "Sam wants to say good night to you."

"He's still up?"

"Yes, Owen. He was asleep, and then he woke up and he wants to talk to you."

"Well great—put him on."

I can literally hear her eyeballs rolling back inside her head. I think they're scraping that part of her brain that used to tell her I was lovable and the eyerolling has slowly chipped away at it over the years. But I don't even care because now I can hear my four-year-old son saying the best word I've ever known: *Dad.*

"Hey, buddy. You out of bed?"

"No. Mom *brung* me the phone." He's so chill for a kid. My son invented low-key excited. But I can tell he's excited to talk to me even though it's only been a couple of hours since I saw him, so I am not going to correct his grammar because I want him to like me.

"Oh, cool. Does the pillow still smell like Grandpa? Is that why you can't sleep?"

My wife hisses at me in the background.

Sam laughs—which is a miracle. He never laughs at me. Maybe my luck is changing. "No. I just *woked* up. I don't know why. It's loud where you are."

"Yeah, I'm in the kitchen at a comedy club, and I have to go work on the stage soon. But hey, do you want to hear a joke about pizza?"

"I guess."

"Aww, never mind—it's too cheesy."

Crickets.

"You get it? Because there's cheese on a pizza. Cheesy."

"Yeah. I get it. Did you make that joke?"

"Depends. Did you think it was funny?"

"Not really."

"Then no, I didn't make that one."

"Good."

"Okay, off to bed, kiddo," my wife says, taking the phone from him.

"Nighty-night," I say.

"He can't hear you," she snaps. "I hope he gets back to sleep. It would be a lot better for him if you didn't have to work so late."

This again. I remember a time when she thought I was funny. When she encouraged me to do stand-up. To pursue my lifelong dream of bringing laughter to the masses instead of making shit tons of money from looking hot in commercials or investing other people's money in mutual funds. Haven't quit my day job as a model yet, but I'm also staying busy enough as a comedian that I don't have to put that finance degree to use either. And yet, somehow, neither of us is happy.

"I'm the headliner, babe. I'm on last."

"I know, Owen. It's great. *For you.* Try not to wake anyone up when you get back."

I'm about to say good night, but she's already hung up.

3

The owner sticks his head into the kitchen, whistles like he's hailing a cab, and signals for me to get out there because the host is about to introduce me.

Time to put on the game face.

"And *that* is why you should always wear pants when you're cooking... Speaking of hot and delicious things that I need to keep my erection away from... Ladies and gentlemen—all the way from Los Angeles, California, and some fancy manscaping spa probably—please give a warm Floridian welcome to the Comedy Den stage... Mr. Owen Brodie!"

I saunter out onto the small stage and pick up the mic, wait for the applause to die down.

It's a full house. I'd rather be pretty much anywhere besides Florida, considering my in-laws live here, but at least my manager was able to get me a gig. Comedy club audiences are usually at least seventy percent male, and the women are usually there on dates. But when my head shot's out front, the crowds skew more female.

And even though I'm off the market as a man, I've learned to work it as a comedian.

"Hello, Tampa. Wow. Thank you. What an incredibly warm and humid welcome. Great-looking audience too. Not as good-looking as I am, but only, like, three percent of humanity is, so good for you."

Pause for awkward laughter.

I think I hear the low chant of a "boooooo" from

the back of the room, but enough people are laughing and clapping that I can't quite make it out.

"Very happy to be in the Sunshine State. I'm here with my wife and son, visiting my in-laws. I feel like if a gator came out of nowhere and started eating me I'd be like, 'Thank you for not casually mentioning how interesting it is that I was getting a finance degree when I first started dating your only daughter and now I'm telling jokes in bars for a living.'"

"Oh my God! A gator joke in Florida, combined with an in-laws joke! This is groundbreaking comedy, people!" a woman yells from the back of the room. I can't see her. There are spotlights in my eyes and the room is dimly lit.

But I'm going to ignore her because I've got over forty minutes of material left to do. Also, she's right. That was a really lame non-joke.

"Being a dad is exhausting." I comb my fingers through my hair thoughtfully. "I used to be handsome." I pause for a moment before deadpanning, "I *still am* handsome. But I used to be too."

That always gets a big laugh when I'm anywhere other than LA or New York. It gets a laugh here, but it also gets that same woman from the back of the club yelling at me.

"Mitch Hedberg called! He wants his joke back!"

That is impressive.

And obnoxious.

But it was indeed an homage to an old Mitch Hedberg joke—good for her.

Usually gets some quiet nods of recognition among other comedians in the audiences in big cities, but this is the first time I've been called out in a place like this.

I ignore her and continue, a little nervous because I'm trying out some new jokes that I don't have a lot of confidence in. But that's what out-of-town gigs are for—trying out shitty new material on people you'll never see again.

"Back when I first started telling people I wanted to do stand-up, they'd tell me I'd never make it—because I'm too handsome and happy to be a comedian. I'd say, 'I'm not that happy. But you think I'm funny enough to make it as a comedian?' and they'd say, 'Oh fuck no. You're not even funny enough to be a funny model.'"

I wait a beat because I know what's coming from the back of the room: "Accurate!"

"I was always the funny one in my family as a kid, just don't ask anyone in my family. Always the class clown in elementary school—big laughs at recess. Then I grew into my face. Suddenly nobody thought it was funny when I farted anymore. They still don't."

Pause for awwws *of feigned condolences from a bunch of women and a few men.*

"Being handsome is okay, I guess. Men want to

punch me. Women want to know what kind of hair product I use. My wife wants to know if she can count on me to bring the right kind of paper towels home from Target this time or if she has to do literally everything herself."

Mild recognition-laughter from the men, and some groans from the ladies.

"Wow! A man complaining about his wife for laughs—he's bringing his A game, everybody!" comes that voice from the back. "Dude—save it for your memoir!"

It's a different voice from the one inside my head that told me not to go this route for tonight's act, but she's saying all the same stuff. I mean, I'm not the Sandra Bullock of good-looking stand-up comics or anything, but I'm always testing the limits of how far I can go with the personal stuff while still being likable and funny. This might be my limit.

Some wonderful person shushes her, but she hisses back, *"You* shush!" And then she yells out, "Hey, Head Shot! Why don't you spend a little less time on crafting your hair and a little more on crafting your jokes!"

Okay.

This woman sounds like what we call in the comedy business—a drunk asshole.

I've got one more thing I want to try out here, so I'm not going to let this chick derail me.

"Seriously, though, I love my wife. Been married

just over four years, with an adorable son who's four years old…" I pause, to let the audience absorb that for a second. Not that these jokes require an understanding of why I got married, but maybe… I don't know—maybe I'm setting up the inevitable future where I'm a divorced single dad comedian. I'd never say that out loud, but after this trip… *Yeesh.* It would break my heart in two, not being able to live with Sam all the time, but…

Yeah, now is not the time to think about it.

"I love being married. When I lived by myself I had this weird feeling I was doing things wrong, and it turns out I was right about *that one thing.* When you're single in college you're an idiot, and that's fine because you're supposed to be an idiot at that age. But nobody wants to be an idiot. So you try out different things. You keep doing things wrong and telling yourself you're learning from your mistakes, but the truth is—that takes too much time. Having a wife saves time. As soon as you get married, there's only one way in the world to do things—you do them the wrong way and then you tell your wife she's right when she informs you how you were supposed to do it."

This is when I pretend my phone's vibrating in my pocket and pull it out to casually check the Caller ID. "Hang on, I better take this." It gets some low-grade laughs. I pretend to answer, placing the microphone back on its stand and muttering into it. "Hey, babe, what's up? I'm in the middle of… Can I call you back in… I just need, like, twenty-five more… Yeah, I can do that… What kind?… Can you just text me the list?… Okay… No, I'll remember." I pull a pen out from my pocket and pretend to write a shopping list on my forearm while holding the phone between my ear and my shoulder. I signal to the audience that I just need one second. "Uh-huh. Original or low fat?… Plain or vanilla?… I do remember, I just wanted to make sure… Uh-huh… Dark chocolate or milk?…" I wink at the audience, like I've got this under control. "You know what, honey, I really have to—okay… Yup. Yeah, I'd love to go to the mall with you and your mom tomorrow morning."

"Oh my gawd! Wrap it up!" the woman in the back calls out. "It stopped being funny eight sentences ago!"

Now, there are two schools of thought among stand-up comics. In the first school, the comic is in charge. You own the stage. The audience paid to come see you, not the other way around. So you always stay in control and don't let the hecklers sway you. That means you ignore them and carry on. In the second school of thought, we do things the right way—we own the stage *and* we let those arrogant little shits know who's boss by heckling them right back.

She sounds pretty young, so she's probably got a lot of sass left in her.

Time to cut her off.

I slide my phone back into my pocket and hold my free hand up over my eyes like a visor. "Sorry—it stopped being funny *eight* sentences ago, you say?"

There's a smattering of laughter when people realize I'm actually responding to that woman. Maybe I'm off my game because of what's going on with my wife. Maybe I'm just not funny. But right now I feel a strange connection with this terrible woman at the back of the room because she's right and she's making me feel more awake and alive than I've felt in weeks. Months, maybe.

I hold my pen up to my arm again like I'm taking notes.

"Well, it was never really very funny, if you want my actual notes," she says, slurring a little.

"Okay, so just cut that whole bit is what you're saying? Any other suggestions?"

"Yeah. Be funnier."

"Got it. Any idea how I could be funnier?"

"Stop being so derivative. Stop being so self-conscious. Be less handsome."

I pretend to write that on my arm and then slip the pen back into my pocket and pick up the mic. "Yeah, I'm not gonna do that. You want to come up here and show me how to be funny, Miss…? Sorry—I didn't get your name."

I cup my hand to my ear, straining to hear her because everyone in the audience is turning to look at her and suddenly she's gone all quiet.

"Lady Hilarious McFunnyPants, did I get that right? Everyone, let's give a warm welcome to the Comedy Den stage—all the way from the back of the room and some dive bar before that probably—Lady Hilarious McFunnyPants, the undisputed queen of jokes!" I gesture for her to come on over, and a lot of people start applauding. A few of them are booing.

I see a shadowy figure standing up back there.

Wow. She's going for it. This should be interesting.

Okay.

Dark hair.

Kind of tall.

Kind of curvy.

A little wobbly but trying hard to maintain her balance and composure.

I don't have a clear view of her, but she's prettier than she sounds.

She's got her handbag with her.

Aaaaand she's leaving.

And flipping me the bird.

"Oh, you're leaving?

And she's gone.

Well, that was anti-climactic.

The audience cheers.

"And she took all the sunshine with her. Maybe next time…"

All the old-guy comedians I've talked to say you can't learn and grow as a comedian unless you've survived bombing on stage. I think I've already grown a lot tonight. And my teacher is probably getting a cab home so she can troll Steve Martin on Twitter.

I feel a little bad that she felt like she had to leave, but...

On with the show.

"Now, where were we?"

1

FRANKIE

Around Three Totally Crappy Years Later

I know I've said this infinity times before, but this time I really mean it: I will never consume alcohol again.

Ever.

Ever.

Ever again.

I will not drink on New Year's Eve.

I will not drink on Super Bowl Sunday with Steve.

Not even if the world should end,

I will not do shots with all my friends…

It certainly feels like it's ending, so I'm just going

to lie here and wait for the zombies to put me out of my misery. I just hope they're really quiet.

I will not mix a Coke with rum.

Why, even cough syrup I will abstain from.

I will not drink mimosas with Mum.

I will not swallow a drunk guy's—

Why is Dr. Seuss writing my thoughts now?

Maybe I'm dead?

If so, this is not the least respectable way for a twenty-six-year-old woman to die in LA. At least I'm wearing pants. I'm wearing everything I was wearing last night, in fact. Including one of my shoes. Minus whatever dignity I still had when yesterday began. It's a relief, really, if I am dead. I will never have to go on a date again. I won't have to find another horrible job to pay the bills. I won't have to go to any more demoralizing cattle calls for tiny parts in awful shows. I won't have to spend another three hours of my life trying to find parking at Trader Joe's. I won't have to pretend to like avocado toast anymore.

Maybe an angel will close the curtains so that fucking Los Angeles morning sun will get out of my fucking face.

Ugh.

Maybe if I try really hard I can telepathically communicate with Mia and get her to come in here to close the curtains.

Nope. I don't think I have any brain cells left.

"Mia…" Shit. Clint Eastwood moved into my

voice box while I was sleeping. I'll never be able to call out to her, and I can't move any part of my body to find my phone.

But miracle of miracles—there's a dainty rap on my bedroom door, and then it opens and Mia pokes her glow-y, smiling face through it. "You're up!"

"*Nuhhh.*"

She lowers her voice. "Sorry."

I snap my eyes shut and point in the general direction of the offending window with the stupid curtains that are letting the shitty sunbeams blast my face.

"Yeah, I'll get that," she whispers.

Most of the time, I wonder if I was some kind of baby-murdering war criminal in my past lives because my karma is pretty terrible. But Mia is one shiny blonde glimmering piece of evidence that I was probably nice to a puppy once or something. Because she's the kindest, most innocent person in Los Angeles and she somehow agreed to let me be her roommate, even though I'm the sort of person who usually wants to throw things at happy people like her.

But I love her a lot, and never more than I do right now because the room is darker and I smell coffee and waffles and bacon.

She has brought me a breakfast tray.

"Can you sit up?" she asks gently.

"It might take me half an hour to lift my head, but I'm going to do it."

"Okay." She giggles. "Take your time. Well, not really, because the coffee and food will get cold. I also brought Advil and water."

"Did you bring breakfast for yourself too?"

"I already had my smoothie and went jogging and showered!"

Of course she did.

I manage to slowly raise my torso up higher than my lower body, and my head isn't throbbing as much up here as it was down there—*no wait, yes it is.*

Mia is holding the bottle of water and the Advil out to me, trying not to smile because she doesn't want to annoy me by being chipper. "You can go ahead and be your happy self," I mutter before tossing the pills into my mouth.

She pulls her phone out from her back pocket, grinning. "Good."

"Question... Did I lick the entire floor of a distillery last night?"

"You don't remember anything?"

I take a sip of coffee and a bite of plain, dry waffle before answering. "I remember bits and pieces of yesterday. I remember getting fired for writing something hilarious and awesome."

"Such bullshit. You should call HR and complain."

"I remember being dumped via text by a guy I didn't even like very much."

"Such an asshole. You're better off without him."

"I remember going to the open mic night and I remember bombing, and the rest is a blur."

She holds up her phone and taps the YouTube app. "But you didn't bomb! You just thought you did. Look—I uploaded the video I shot of your set, and it already had five likes and six comments this morning!"

Mia acts as though she's my assistant, even though I never hired her and I certainly don't pay her, but she set up a YouTube account for me as a comedian because she wants me to get discovered. This is all just so I can afford to move out of her apartment and she never has to see me again, I think. "How many of the comments were my mother?"

"Only four of them. And they were all positive! Look—you've had thirty-seven views already and seven likes! Watch the video—you were really funny."

I hate seeing myself on camera, and the sound of my recorded voice makes me cringe. But I take the phone from her and watch the video anyway because I don't have the energy to argue with a positive person who's trying to cheer me up right now.

It was my first time signing up for open mic at this legendary bar and grill on Sunset. Normally, I would never get up and tell jokes while people are eating unless I was getting paid, but I'd just gotten fired and dumped, so I was like—fuck it, let's see if this day can get any worse. And it is still my belief that it did.

The place was half full of mostly middle-aged rocker types. Not really my target audience, but I had already had a beer and a half by the time I took the stage, so it didn't matter. Mia was slapping one hand on the tabletop and yelling "Yay, Frankie!" while holding her phone up to film me, and maybe five other people clapped. But I still looked fairly upbeat and my hair looked less terrible than usual.

I placed my ukulele on top of the stool, took the microphone from the stand, and just launched right into it: "Hey, thank you so much. Anyone here living happily ever after with the love of their life? Anyone? Anyone? You, sir? Is that your wife you're holding hands with? She's lovely. Your wife's at home? Never mind."

That got a few laughs.

"So I'm super happy for everyone who's married and stuff, but I just got dumped by yet another boyfriend. I would sincerely love to be one of those girls who's all..." And this is where I started mumble-singing into the mic.

"And I will always be grateful for the five times you
attempted
cunnilingus
and that time you brought me a red velvet cupcake
even though I prefer carrot cake

but whatever, thanks for everything, let's be friends foreverrrrr!

"But I'm way more like…"

And then I placed the mic back on the stand, picked up my ukulele, strummed a few chords just for effect, stored the ukulele between my legs, and basically yelled into the mic in the key of mid-'90s Alanis Morrissette.

"I want you to know that I faked every orgasm I ever had with you
I hope the next girl finally teaches you how to kiss
and where the clitoris is
and where the G-spot is actually located
I mean your butt looks great in jeans, I guess
And you have pretty good taste in music
But fuck you, asshole—your show is overrated
And you're way too opinionated
about dumb things like socks
And you never appreciated it
when I blew you!
And by the way, you left your vintage Star Wars T-shirt at my place
and I'm keeping it because you're a fake nerd and it fits me!"

And then I strummed the ukulele again, and you can hear Mia laughing and slapping the tabletop, bless her big, beautiful heart. I put the uke back down on the stool, held the mic again, and started pacing around a bit on the tiny stage area.

"Little bit about me—I've dated nine different guys named Justin. After every breakup with every guy, no matter what his name is, my girlfriends get all Lizzo on my ass and they're like, 'Baby, we goin out. That man no longer exists on this planet, and if you don't believe me—ask these five shots of tequila.' I put on a huge pair of hoop earrings, crop top, faux-leather pants, and five-inch heels. I attempt eyeliner and then remove it because fuck you, eyeliner. I put on a hat that I bought at the flea market, but my roommate's like, 'Mmmm. No.'"

And then Mia went "Woohoooo!" from behind the shaky camera because I talked about her in my act and she was hoping I wouldn't notice that she was basically the only person in the place who was paying attention to me.

I continued with my bit. "In the Uber on the way to the club, in my mind I look like Alicia Keys, and in my heart I know that this badass, ragtag gang of female dorks are all I really need in life. And then I make out with the first guy who talks to me, post a selfie of myself HAVING THE BEST TIME EVER-RRRRR on Insta, and then I vomit into a public toilet (if I'm lucky) and get my hand stuck in one of my hoop earrings. And then I leave early, go home by myself barefoot—because fuck you, five-inch heels. And then I order pizza, cry while watching whatever Bill Murray movie is on Netflix—because why can't everyone be him?"

That's when a few random people finally acknowledged my existence by cheering, and you can just see from the expression on my face how surprised and grateful I was. It's so sad.

"Yeah! Bill Murray! Am I right?"

Silence. I had them for one second, and then I lost them again.

That's where the YouTube video cuts—very abruptly—to me doing a bunch of random Bill Murray impressions, including my personal favorite from *Ghostbusters*: "We came. We saw. We kicked its ass!" And they got laughs. I don't remember what it felt like to get those laughs, unfortunately, but it's nice to see it on YouTube, I guess.

"What did you cut out?"

Mia waves her hand dismissively and takes her phone from me. "Nothing. My phone was shaking so much because I was laughing, so I cut that part out." She isn't looking at me because she's a terrible liar. "Did you hear how loud everyone was laughing at your impressions? You totally killed."

"Mia. What did you edit out?"

"It wasn't bad…" She touches her hand to my knee. "You just looked so sad and dejected. It looked like you were having a private moment, that's all.

Didn't seem like something that should be on the internet."

Yeah. *That* I remember feeling.

I pat her hand. "I think that was the moment I decided to quit doing stand-up."

"Yeah. But you're not going to."

She's not wrong. Stand-up comedy is the emotionally unavailable Heath Ledger to my gay cowboy Jake Gyllenhaal. I wish I knew how to quit it.

"Where's my phone?"

Mia gets up and goes over to my dresser to retrieve it for me. "Right here. I plugged it in for you last night."

I pop the last bit of waffle into my mouth and mumble, "I don't even know how I'd live without you. Here, you can have my bacon. I don't think my stomach's ready for non-carbs yet."

The first thing I see on my phone screen is a voicemail notification from my mum. She left the message about two hours ago, which would have been seven o'clock in Tampa.

"I got a voice message from Donna," I tell Mia, imitating my mum's Australian accent.

"Ooooh, can I hear?!" Mia claps, all excited.

This should be fun because Donna Hogan gets especially Aussie when she's upset. I play the voice-mail and put it on speakerphone.

"Hello, darling. Just got your email. Listen—it's

fucked you got sacked, but let's not chuck a wobbly, all right?… Hang on." She doesn't pull the phone away from her mouth when she yells at my dad. Ever. "*Peetah! Peetah! Peetah!* Turn down the telly. I'm talking to our *dawdah*!… No, it's a message! Just turn it off, will ya?!… Your dad says hey, and we're sending a check for a few hundred *dollahs* to help you out. Call Uncle *Mahtin*! I know you're too proud to ask for help, but that's what relatives are for. Especially *Mahtin*, that little shit. I'm guessing you were on the piss last night, so don't forget to drink your *wohhdah*. Oh, and I thought of a very funny joke story for you—about not being able to find anything to watch on Netflix! Love you."

"Well, that should be good." My mum regularly sends me ideas for jokes, and instead of actually writing them as jokes, I just imitate her telling me about her joke ideas in my act.

"What's 'on the piss?'" Mia asks, giggling.

"Drinking alcohol."

"She's so cute! Are you going to call your uncle Martin?"

"No way."

"Say hi to him for me if you do…" She's blushing. God help her.

"I can't ask him for help. I just can't."

I close the app and am about to text my mum to tell her I'm not going to beg her little brother, who just happens to be a big important talent manager, for a job and that I don't want them to send me money—but I see a notification from Twitter that Owen Brodie just tweeted.

"Oh my God. Owen Brodie tweeted yet another lame joke five minutes ago, and he already has nine hundred likes."

"He's so cute..." Mia says, nibbling on a piece of bacon and watching me for a reaction.

"He is not cute! He's obnoxiously handsome, and he should have stuck to modeling."

"I love his brother. He's such a good actor. And gorgeous. But Owen's funny."

I scoff at that. "Barely. The guy's been doing stand-up for as long as I have. He's a headliner, he's done a Netflix comedy special, and he just got some development deal to do a series for a new streaming platform. For him to star in. Meanwhile, I'm still doing open mics and copywriting for horrible corporations."

She sighs. "Well...not anymore. You were fired."

"I hate the world. I don't know why it bothers me so much that he's so successful as a comedian. It just does."

"I have some ideas as to why it bothers you so much."

Ignoring her, I reread Owen's stupid tweet.

Owen Brodie @theowenbrodie

I don't want to brag or anything, but I'm really popular with my mom.

I mean, it's cute and random and I can see why people would like it, but…

Frankie Hogan @frankiesayrelax
Replying to @theowenbrodie
I don't want to brag or anything, but that's not what yer mom told me last night…

Ahhh, classic response.

Now I feel a little better.

Not my finest work, but… Shit, that doesn't even make sense.

Who cares—he always ignores me anyway. Asshole.

"You are a tad obsessed with him though."

"No I'm not."

"Okay."

"I'm not."

"No, I know. But you should probably check your direct messages from last night. Is there a way to delete the ones you sent?"

Whaaaaaaaat?

I open up the DMs in my Twitter app. The most recent conversation is with Owen Brodie.

"Ohhhhhh no no no no no no nooooooo."

ME: *Just <bomb emoji> my open <microphone emoji>. Hope you're happy, head shot.*
ME: *<woman shrugging emoji> why I blame you for everything but I do.*
ME: *Your probably won't even see these message but whatever. I guess I just want to say that I respect how you handling me in Tampa that time I heckled you.*
ME: *I mean I was made at you for three years but I'm over it now. I was an asshole but at least you held my attention and made people laugh. I think people most laugh because you hot but whatever. It's something.*
ME: *Good luck with your series. It sounds cute. I don't even mean that sarcastic. Stand-up is hard. Really hard. I give up.*
ME: *Also I didn't mean what I say that time about your haircut in that new profile pic. It's hot. I like how your hair stands up it's really friendly and it make your blue eyes shinier or somethings <woman shrugging emoji>*
ME: *But get over yourself.*

"Mia! Why'd you let me do this?"

"It seemed really important to you last night. Also, you growled at me when I told you to stop."

"How do I delete them?! If I delete them, does that delete it for him too or just on my end?"

"I think it's just on your side."

"Wow. Shit. Fuck. Well. Hopefully he won't even see the messages. I mean, he may have blocked me years ago for all I know. Right?"

She nods enthusiastically. "Hopefully!"

I look back down at my phone, about to close the app, but...a new message has popped up in the conversation. That stupidly handsome, grinning face with the friendly, erect hair follicles and shiny blue eyes is right there, taunting me.

"Oh my God."

"What?!"

OWEN BRODIE: *Had a feeling you were the girl from Tampa. Always wanted to tell you that you were right about everything you said that night. That material wasn't funny. But I survived bombing and so will you. Don't give up stand-up. You seem funny. Totally unlikable. But funny. Everyone bombs. Builds character. Onward and upward (like my hair). Hope you're feeling okay this morning. Hang in there. ;)*

"Oh my God!"

"What?! Did he write back?"

The tingly rollercoaster-drop feeling in my lower abdomen and upper lady bits area has got to be hangover-related and not Owen Brodie-related. But it's real. And it's not going away.

"He winky-faced me."

Mia gasps. "Emoji or emoticon?"

"Emoticon."

She exhales, relieved. "Good. That's way hotter."

"It's not hot. He was being condescending."

"Winky-face emoticon is flirty!"

"No it isn't."

"It is! He's divorced, you know. He's legally single."

"Of course I know. Being a divorced single dad is all part of his act now. So I'm told."

"Write him back! Winky-face him back!"

"No way. He'll think I like him. He is literally the poster boy for everything that is wrong with this business."

"Okay, then maybe don't write anything back at all."

She tries to take the phone from me, but I growl at her.

ME: *To be clear--I AM funny, I do NOT think you are hot and I already had character.*

"What'd you say? Were you nice?"

"No."

"Frankie." She frowns at me.

I huff. "Fine."

ME: *Thank you for acknowledging how correct I was about your awful jokes in Tampa. <winking face emoji>*

I drop my phone like it's hot. "Shit. I winky-faced him."

"Emoticon or emoji?"

"Emoji."

Mia grimaces.

"Now he's going to think I'm flirting with him."

"Good!"

"The opposite of good! Shit. I'm still a little drunk, I think." I delete the Twitter app from my phone. "There. I'm going back to sleep. Thank you for breakfast. I love you."

"Love you."

I bury myself under the covers.

I'm never drinking alcohol again.

And I'm never doing stand-up again.

And I'm never going on Twitter again.

And I might never get out of bed again.

But, shit… I have to get a new job.

And I wonder what he meant by that winky-face emoticon.

2

OWEN BRODIE JOKE NOTEBOOK - JUNE

Is this joke-worthy?...

- Is it bad social media etiquette to hate-jerk it to someone's Twitter profile pic when you don't follow her back or "like" her incredibly obnoxious troll tweets that you secretly find funny?

- If that woman who heckled you in Tampa three years ago keeps crashing your fantasies to criticize you for being too handsome and hilarious while she's dressed like Princess Leia in Return of the Jedi *and chained to the foot of your bed—does that mean you should retweet her @replies occasionally?*

* Yeah, the second one might be a little too specific, and it's bad enough I have to be on Twitter, so why would I want to talk about it in my act?

. . .

- When you're divorced and you start dating again, you carry around this secret shameful list of all the things your ex-wife hated about you. I thought I'd be all excited to start over. I thought it would be a blank slate and I'd be like—every woman is going to come in their pants as soon as they meet me! When I fuck them with my newly freed, superhuman sexual powers and do all the filthy, awesome things I wasn't allowed to do to my ex-wife to them, they will be so grateful for how good I made them feel that they will make me a sandwich and then throw me a parade. They will not be mad at me if I don't show up to that parade because I already had a show scheduled at a club. And then when I see them later, they'll wear crop tops and short shorts while giving me a super casual but hot hand job while we watch the Weather Channel on my big screen, and then they'll go home even before I ask them to leave and not complain about it because that is how amazing of a kisser I am.

But now when I meet someone I kind of like, I'm all, "Yo, sup gurl, ride my pony." But in the back of my mind I'm thinking: I will ultimately disappoint you by being a selfish human who is driven by a need for public approval through laughter and applause and who also doesn't like the same TV shows you like. I will probably not like anyone in your entire extended family, and I won't be able to pretend that I don't think they're humorless, small-minded assholes who spoiled you rotten and always vote for the wrong political party.

* Okay. Not funny. I should probably stick with stuff about being a single dad. Like how the criteria for seriously dating a woman now has become: Is she comfortable knowing that she will be joked about on stage after our inevitable breakup? Does she find me unbelievably sexy because I have wet wipes in my glove compartment? Is she open to booty calls that revolve around my co-parenting schedule, and will she sit through entire episodes of Spider-man *and nature shows that seven-year-olds probably shouldn't be allowed to watch? And will she give me a quick hand job in the bathroom while my son is watching wild animals kill each other in slow motion?*

* It really sucks that my contract for the show stipulates a morality clause for my stand-up act. Bob Saget was allowed to do filthy stand-up while he was on Full House. *But, as my agent, manager, and lawyer explained —that was before the internet. Now if you're playing a TV dad on a family show and you do a blue stand-up act, somebody could post a video online that night and conservative parents would be petitioning the network the next morning. And for subscription streaming services, the threat is even more dire.*

So I'll have to keep my filthy thoughts to myself for now.

Like the ones I keep having about @frankiesayrelax — who should really respond to that last message I sent her.

I should start a troll account called @frankieneedas-

panking. Or @frankiewantapearlnecklace. Or @heckler-wantmypecker

Bet she'd "like" my tweets.

But yeah.

Too many characters for a Twitter handle.

Better keep it to myself.

3

OWEN

I'm pretty sure the movie score to my son's life is a cello solo with occasional trombone *wah wah wah wahhh* sounds, and that breaks my heart. All kids should have joyful trumpets and drums and calliopes and I don't know…ukuleles as their soundtrack. That is why, after picking Sam up at my ex-wife's house, I immediately brought him to the nearest frozen yogurt place for a treat. Because Ashley told me not to let him eat any ice cream for dessert because she wants him to lose a little weight.

Fuck that.

My boy's gonna eat a giant cardboard bowl full of frozen pseudo-healthy dairy topped with literally anything he wants. If he wants a pound of M&Ms on top of four swirls, covered with whipped cream and an ice cream cake, I'm buying it for him. It'll give him an epic tummy ache, but he's allowed to eat all of it if he wants to. That's good parenting, and fuck anyone who says otherwise. I'll make him eat a carrot and give him a gummy vitamin when we get home, or whatever.

I have him for the week—and I'm so glad—but I've got a show tonight, and his nanny was supposed to come with us to look after him for a couple of hours. When I got to Ashley's house in Brentwood, she informed me that the nanny would be staying there with the new baby tonight because she and her husband have an event to go to. Why can't I just come back to pick Sam up later tonight, you ask? *Because everyone's life doesn't have to revolve around my schedule anymore.* Why did she not give me a heads-up so I could make alternate arrangements, one might wonder? *Because she's been so busy with the baby all day and she had to go shopping for an evening gown that fits her—not that I would understand what it's like to not be able to fit into your favorite dresses after giving birth.*

Over two years since we were officially divorced —you'd think she'd be blaming her new husband for everything by now. But nope. I swear, she would divorce me again if she could, as long as she didn't have to marry me again first.

But honestly, I don't even care about all that. I'm worried about Sam. Summer break has started. He should be having fun, but I can just tell that ever since the baby was born, he isn't getting enough attention when he stays with them. They all mean well, I get it. I'm probably projecting some forgotten feelings I had when I was three years old and my little brother Dylan came along.

That little shit.

I open the door to the pastel-colored frozen yogurt place for Sam. "You excited, buddy?"

He shrugs. "I mean, it's frozen yogurt, but sure."

That was like getting a fucking standing ovation from this kid.

The blonde behind the cash register turns and gives us an impossibly bright smile. "Hello, gentlemen! Welcome to Froyoville—population *you*!"

"Say hi to the nice lady, Sam."

"I don't want to say hi to people. I just want dessert."

"Fair enough."

The young lady giggles. "Well lemme know if you have any questions or need any help with anything."

"I think we got this, thanks."

I get Sam all set up with his vanilla—seriously, what kid asks for low-fat vanilla—with granola and chocolate chip topping. He must have heard his mom talking about putting him on a diet. He's barely overweight. She just wants him to have a six-pack. Meanwhile, she was always mad at me for spending time at the gym.

But I'm not going to think about that right now.

I'm not going to get mad while I'm here with my kid.

And I need to find a fucking babysitter for tonight, or I'm screwed.

I pull out a chair for my boy and sit down opposite him at a little table by the wall of windows.

"You aren't gonna get anything?"

"Nahhh. I'm too uncultured for yogurt."

He stares at me, blank-faced. Doesn't even blink.

"You get it?"

"No."

"It's a joke. Because yogurt is cultured milk."

He shakes his head and digs into his yogurt.

"*Fro-yo* information, that was a very sophisticated and super funny joke."

"Oh-kayyy." I get an eye-roll. Seems to me I shouldn't have to deal with eye-rolls from my kid until he's thirteen, but at least it's a reaction.

"You'll get it in about fifteen or twenty years, and when you do—I want you to call me. Or however people get in touch with each other in the future. Just be sure to let me know the minute you realize how funny your old man is."

"Uh-huh. I'll let you know, Dad."

I am this close to pulling up *Entertainment Weekly*'s rave review of my stand-up act from a couple of months ago on my phone and showing it to him. That's how badly I need the validation from this particular person. I mean, it's not just about wanting my son to think I'm funny—I want to make him happy. I would saw off my own arm right now if it would make him laugh. It's not like he never laughs. I've seen him with other kids and he's always having a blast. He just doesn't laugh at *me*.

I can't wait till he's in college—maybe even when he's old enough to drive—and I can start telling him awesome classic jokes like: A woman goes into the dry cleaner's, and the old guy inspects the stain on the skirt she brought in. She asks him if he can get the stain out, but he's hard of hearing and he says, "Come again?" And she says, "No, this time it's yogurt."

I watch Sam carefully dip the spoon into his dessert so that he gets equal amounts of both kinds of toppings and frozen yogurt in each bite, and then he shoves it into his mouth, barely chewing. He seems satisfied though. So that's good.

Now I just have to find a fucking babysitter for tonight, drop my kid off wherever I need to during rush hour, and then get out to Hollywood to do a set before driving back to pick him up from wherever.

I'm about to call my neighbor, Mrs. Billings, who's looked after him before, but then I remember seeing her daughter over there to water her plants because Mrs. Billings is out of town.

So I call my older brother Miles on his personal cell phone, though he's probably still at the office.

He's a hotshot entertainment lawyer, but he does make time to respond to family texts and calls. He usually responds with a reminder of how busy he is and some snarky comment, but he's almost always available. And he is also a divorced single dad with a kid, so we try to help each other out whenever possible. It would be great if our kids didn't despise each other, but what are ya gonna do.

Miles answers on the third ring. I can hear NPR in the background, which means he's driving. "Yeah? I've got a conference call with a client in four minutes."

I speak really slowly to piss him off. "I was just calling to tell you that I love you."

"Fuck off. What do you need?"

"I just picked Sam up, and I have a gig tonight."

Sam looks up, eyes filled with horror. "Not Macy!" He has hated his cousin since they were babies. It's adorable.

I wink at him.

"Awww, sorry, man. I'm on my way to pick Macy up at her dance class, and then I'm taking her to see *Annie* at the Ahmanson."

"You mean the show she didn't get cast in or even get a callback for?"

"Yeah, we don't talk about that. I'm pretty sure she's just going to boo at all the child actors, but maybe she'll suddenly become a super chill, supportive, noncompetitive person in the next hour. We'll see."

No comment. "So can I borrow your nanny?"

"It's her night off. She's celebrating her thirtieth wedding anniversary with her family."

We're silent for, like, three seconds, and I know without a doubt that we're both wondering how anyone manages to stay married for that long and what the hell is wrong with us that neither of us could keep a marriage alive for more than four years. But we would never say these things out loud to each other. Not sober anyway.

"Well, that doesn't sound anywhere near as fun or emotionally satisfying as what I have planned."

"Same," he says. "I almost feel sorry for her."

"Well, I gotta go. There's a line of, like, fifty women waiting to talk to me."

"Yeah, a bunch of women in a Prius just threw their panties at me, so I should say hi to them, or something."

"Go get 'em, tiger."

"Don't break too many hearts tonight."

I hang up and say to Sam reassuringly, "Not Macy."

"Phew!" He goes back to inhaling his dessert.

The truth is, he probably doesn't even care whose TV or iPad he gets parked in front of for a couple of hours. He'll probably just sleep. But times like this I really wish my parents had stayed in LA instead of moving back to Texas a few years ago.

"Can I stay with Uncle Dylan?" Sam asks, all hopeful. He loves and idolizes my little brother. Which is sweet but also deeply annoying.

"Lemme see if he's around." I text him because he never answers his phone. Little shit.

ME: *You in town?*
DYLAN: *That depends which town you're referring to.*
ME: *Los Angeles. I need someone to look after Sam for a couple of hours.*
DYLAN: *I'm still in New York. Starring in a Broadway play that the New York Times reviewer called "Riveting and thoroughly entertaining...despite Dylan Brodie's somewhat mannered performance."*
ME: *Oh yeah. I saw that review. That was funny.*
DYLAN: *Kindly go fuck yourself.*
ME: *That's a solid Friday night plan for me. I deserve a kindly fuck for a change. Thought you'd be back by now. Has your costar dumped you yet?*
DYLAN: *No. We're still very much in love. She might move to LA to be with me. Or maybe I'll move here. I don't even care where we are. I just want to be with her. This is real.*
ME: *Uh-huh.*
DYLAN: *Fuck you. I gotta get back onstage. Say hey to my buddy for me.*

ME: *Yeah, break a leg and please accept my condolences in advance for when yet another leading lady breaks your sad little heart.*
DYLAN: *<raised middle finger emoji>*
ME: *<face blowing a kiss emoji>*

I scrub my face with the palm of my hand. "Uncle Dylan's in New York right now."

"Can I go there?"

"No."

"Why not?"

"Because it takes five and a half hours to fly to New York. I need to find someone to look after you tonight."

"Why can't Blanca look after me?"

"Because she's going to be busy."

"Doing what?"

I take a long, deep breath before answering. I don't want to be short with my kid just because my ex-wife is being a dick. "I don't know, buddy. I just know I have to find someone else."

There is only one other person I can think of right now, and that's my friend Shane Miller. Dylan played his younger brother on a Disney Channel show called *That's So Wizard* back when they were teenagers. Back when Dylan wasn't a pretentious actor who takes himself too seriously. Now Shane's attached to direct the pilot episode of the family show I have in development—the one that neither of

us would have gotten involved with if we took
ourselves too seriously.

ME: *SOS. Single dad emergency. Is your scary nanny
busy tonight?*
SHANE: *If your single dad emergency involves wanting
to date my sixty-something scary nanny, I will just tell
you right now that after the last time you guys were here,
she told me, "I do not trust a man with that kind of chin."*
ME: *Well, that is disappointing, but I actually need
someone to babysit Sam for a couple of hours while I'm at
a gig in Hollywood. Thought maybe if she has the night
off, I could pick her up and bring her to my place. I could
throw on a high neck turtleneck, hide my chin with it.*
SHANE: *Oh man I'm sorry. The twins are with Margo,
so she's over there this week. But Willa and I are at home
with the baby. Sam can hang with us.*
ME: *That is so nice of you to offer, but I can't ask you to
do that. It's cool. I'll figure it out.*
SHANE: *Ok, lemme know if you change your mind. See
you on the Zoom meeting next week.*
ME: *Right. Is it too soon to clear a space on our mantles
for all the Emmys we're going to win for this?*
SHANE: *Not at all! I've already advised my wife to start
calling me "multiple Emmy-winning actor-director Shane
Miller." Have a great gig. I'll probably never make it to
one of your shows, but just know that I support you. xo*
ME: *Thanks! I'll probably only ever watch your movies if
I'm on a plane and there's no other option. xoxo*

I guess now the only question is… Do I call the owner of the comedy club to ask him if it's okay to bring my seven-year-old son and have him hang out in his office while I'm on stage? Or do I just show up with my kid to a twenty-one-and-over venue that has a two-drink-minimum and make him tell me no to my face twenty minutes before I have to go on?

"Hey. I've got a fun idea."

He grins. "Do I get to go to New York to stay with Uncle Dylan?"

"No. He's too busy with work to look after you. How about you come with me to my show tonight? You'll probably have to stay in the back office because kids aren't supposed to be there, but there's Wi-Fi so you can watch stuff on your iPad."

He shrugs. "Okay. Will there be a sofa for me to nap on?"

"Yes." *I don't even want to know what kind of action that sofa has seen though. A lot of "yogurt stains"…* "Remind me to grab a blanket from home on the way. To put over the sofa so you don't have to actually touch the sofa."

"Why?"

"Because. You're not even a little excited to see where I go to work?"

"I guess. A little." He grins again.

This kid. He's egging me on, like a chick.

And that just makes me think of @frankiesayrelax.

And I need to stop thinking about her.

And I definitely need to stop checking to see if she's replied to my message yet.

Sam swallows another mouthful of froyo and then asks, "When are you going away?"

"I'm not going away, buddy."

He looks up at me, frowning, and blinks at me like I'm an idiot.

"Oh, you mean for my stand-up tour? That's in two weeks actually."

"How long are you going away for?"

"A month. One month. I'll be going all across the country. But I can call you and FaceTime you every day if you want."

He stares down at his plastic spoon and nods once.

"Do you want me to call and FaceTime you every day? Because I will."

"Sure, I guess."

I swear I can actually hear the cello solo in his head right now. He is disappearing into his thoughts now, and I don't want to lose him.

"Hey. Sam."

His eyes flick up to meet mine.

"How'd you like to go on my stand-up tour with me?"

I don't have a fucking clue how I'm going to swing this if he says yes, but there's a glimmer of something in those blue eyes now. Something that resembles excitement. Like he might actually be thrilled to be able to spend a month on the road with his dad.

"Will we go to New York to see Uncle Dylan?!"

Yup. Just like a chick.

4

FRANKIE

Possibly the only thing more disheartening than working at a crappy job in LA—when all you really want to do is the thing that you moved out here to do—is looking at listings for new crappy jobs because you keep getting fired from the other ones.

I've already gone through the current industry job list, and I know it would just be a waste of time to apply to be an assistant again. It's not that I don't have the right kind of personality to do whatever someone tells me to do simply because they're paying me. It's that the people who tell me to do things for them have the right kind of personality for dictators and the wrong kind of personality for engaging with people who have a sense of humor and find their narcissism boring but also really funny.

I am also not sure that I should write for another company that doesn't think outside the box.

I am starting to think that I should just be a waitress, even though I'm not very good at carrying things while I walk. Or being friendly to strangers. Or being around food without eating it.

But maybe I can get a job where I work with dogs! The kind of job where I literally only have to work with dogs though. Not their owners or potential owners or people who've rescued them. That's gotta be a thing, right? Homeless dogs need to be walked and groomed too. I just don't think they'd pay very well.

My phone buzzes, and my body tenses up because I've seen too many movies and TV shows where characters who are unemployed get calls from debt collectors. I pay my bills. I have no reason to be afraid of my phone. Aside from the fact that I hate talking on the phone because I'm not sixty.

The Caller ID tells me it's my uncle Martin's office.

Which means my mother told him I lost my job and need help. Again.

Which means I'm going to have to tell him why I lost the other job.

Which is going to suck.

I clear my throat and attempt to answer the phone like someone who is living her best life while hanging out with people who are also living their best lives and laughing about it because we're all so happy and successful.

"Hahahahahaha—hello?!"

"Hello... Is this Frankie Hogan?"

"Yes."

"Oh. That didn't sound like you. I thought maybe I called the wrong number," says my uncle's assistant.

"No, it's me. I'm doing great—how are *you*?"

Except you didn't ask, but whatever.

"Totally. I have Martin Hancock calling for you. Can you hold?"

"Sure, I'll take that call *and* I'll hold."

"Great. He'll be so happy to hear it. He's just finishing up with a client. Hang on."

And then I get to hear the on-hold music that is designed to cheer you up and make you forget that Hollywood is a soulless industry that you are desperately trying to be an important part of while trying not to appear desperate or interested at all.

I hate being the troubled niece. My mum's younger brother is a hotshot talent manager at a big, shiny management company. He specializes in representing comedians, which you'd think would be great for me, but it's incredibly awkward. His clients are all big glittering stars of comedy—not the terrible ones either. He took me to lunch at a private club called Soho House when I first moved here a couple of years ago. The restaurant was filled with celebrities just hanging out, no big deal, meanwhile I shamelessly ordered half the menu and wrapped up the warm bread to take home with me. That was when he told me—very nicely—that he wouldn't be able to help me directly as a comedian but he will always help out with day jobs and money if I'm ever in dire need of it to pay the bills.

He's gotten me three jobs since then, and I've been fired from all of them. For being too hilarious and awesome. Most recently for being a junior copywriter that is way too hilarious and awesome for a supposedly hip and fun live entertainment conglomerate that sells tickets to overpriced shows performed by overrated entertainers of all kinds.

I just need to figure out how to sell this to Martin, who is mostly cool but also probably not convinced that I'm as hilarious and awesome as I seem to think I am.

Mia thinks my uncle is hot. Obviously I don't see him that way. I happen to think Crocodile Dundee is hot, but Uncle Martin is, like, *get away with wearing a velvet suit with a T-shirt and loafers* kind of hot.

"Frankie, you there?"

"G'day, Uncle Marty."

He sighs, and I can hear him scrubbing his stubbly, tanned, poreless face. "What do I always tell you, kid? *Nevah evah* call me *Mahty*."

"But that's your name. *Mahty* Hancock."

This has been our schtick ever since I was a

teenager. Do I only call him that because it pisses him off and it sounds like *mighty hand cock*? Yes. That is why I do it, and people should be paying me to have the sense of humor of a twelve-year-old boy instead of sighing and scrubbing their faces at me. That is one of the many, many things on my list of things that is wrong with this world.

"Yeah, let's cut to the chase, shall we?"

"Sure! My roommate Mia says hi, by the way."

"Oh yeah?... G'day, Mia."

"She's not here right now, but don't flirt with my roommate. That's gross."

"I wasn't flirting. That's just how I am."

"Yeah. You're gross."

"Listen, kid. Donna told me you need a job. What happened to the copywriting gig I got you?"

Deep breath, here goes...

"Great question! You know how it was my job as a copywriter to come up with innovative ways to help the company promote events on digital fan-facing platforms?"

"Uh-huh..."

"Well, the most innovative way to promote a stadium concert for a certain young male pop star was to highlight how entitled and talentless he is because clearly only people who hate themselves and have no taste in music would want to attend the concert of a spoiled brat who's been insulting to his fans, abusive to his ex-girlfriends, and is probably still an asshole even though he claims to be making amends by posting apologies on social media."

Another epic sigh, followed by more audible face-scrubbing. "Right."

"I'm not saying they were wrong for firing me, but somebody had to say it."

"Okay, kid. Believe it or not, I do care more about you and my *sistah* than I do about my contacts at a live entertainment company. But maybe twenty-six is a bit too old for someone to be a little shit—you think?"

"I'm pretty sure I'll be able to pull this off for the rest of my life actually."

"We'll see about that. Here's why I called—one of my clients, Owen Brodie, needs a short-term nanny for his kid."

"Say what now?"

"A nanny. Is that not how they pronounced it in Florida? *Nawnny?* A *caretakah* for his child."

"No, I know what a nanny is. Since when is Owen Brodie your client?"

"'Bout a year now, I think. He had a fuckwit manager before me. You know him?"

"Not personally."

"He's funny."

I have to literally bite my tongue to stop myself from saying *not really.*

"He's starting a month-long cross-country tour soon, and he wants to take his seven-year-old son with him. He'll need someone to look after Sam occasionally before they leave town too, actually. He ended up having to take the kid with him to the Comedy Shop this weekend when he did his set. And he *bahfed* on the rug in the owner's office."

I am way too pleased to hear this. "Owen Brodie barfed at the Comedy Shop?!"

"No. His son did."

"Oh."

That is very disappointing.

"Anyway, he's in a bit of a fix. None of the nannies from the agencies are willing to travel for an entire month. But you would be, right?"

"I mean…yes?"

"And you've looked after kids before, I told him, right?"

"I paid for half of my tuition with the money I made from babysitting."

"Well, you'd be making more than any of the other jobs you've had because you'll basically have to be available to look after Sam at all times. Owen would pay for your meals and accommodations, and he can pay for medical benefits. For approximately a month and a half."

"That is very generous. So this is a headlining tour? Like what, at comedy clubs or at theater venues?"

"Theaters. He's already sold-out in some cities."

I'm not jealous I'm not jealous I'm not jealous.

I need a job I need a job I need a job.

Just because Owen Brodie is an unfunny, overrated, overly handsome asshat, that doesn't mean I won't like his seven-year-old son.

"Well, that is so great for him. I guess I'd have to meet his son. To make sure we don't hate each other. His son and me, I mean."

"Yeah, of course. My office will set that up for you. I've met his kid actually. He's a good kid. Grumpy little arsehole. But funny. Likes to take naps. He's got red hair like his mum. He's basically *Gahfield*, but without the fur. Or the tail. Or four paws. Probably likes lasagna, though."

"Marty! You can't say that about a child. That's so mean."

"It's not mean. You'll see. And stop calling me *Mahty*. Listen, I know it's not your dream job, but you'll be around a successful comedian, so you might learn a thing or two. Most likely make some new contacts through him on the road. You interested or not?"

"I'm interested. Have you, uhhhh, have you already told him my name?"

"I think I just called you my niece, Frankie. Why?"

"Nothing. He's probably assuming my last name is Hancock."

"Yeah, my assistant will give him your information."

54

"No, don't! I mean, you can give him my email address, but I don't really want men I don't know to have my full name and phone number."

"Owen is my client, and he's a good guy."

"I'll be the judge of that."

He sighs once again, long and loud, and I feel his frustration deep in my soul. "Listen, kid. I know you're a talented person, and I want you to succeed. But this is the last time I'm gonna help you get a job. I know it sucks to be where you are in life when it seems like every undeserving arsehole around you is doing *bettah* than you. But you need to fix that attitude. We all have to pay our dues, but nobody wants to fall on their sword for a cynic. Y'know?"

The hot sting of tough love is making my eyes water.

I don't even seem to have a snarky comeback.

So I guess...I *do* know.

"Yeah. I know. I do really appreciate your—"

"What? Hang on, hang on." He puts me on hold for three seconds before hopping back on with me. "Kid, I gotta go. Dave Chappelle's on the other line."

"Oh, give him my love. I gotta go too—Tina Fey's trying to FaceTime me."

"I'll have my assistant email you about the meeting with Owen and the kid."

"Thank you. I really appreciate it, Uncle Martin."

"Sure. Just promise me you won't be too... y'know...*you*."

"I will do my best. Or someone else's best, I suppose."

He doesn't respond because he's already hung up on me so he can talk to Chappelle.

Which is fine.

Or maybe it's terrible.

Maybe I should call him back immediately because there is no way in hell Owen Brodie will want to hire me when he finds out who I am.

And if he does want to hire me—well then, what does that say about *him*?

And do I really want to have to look at his face all day every day for over a month?

Oh, but maybe his adorable son just needs someone to love him while his dad's telling awful jokes to crowds of people who just want to look at him.

I stare down at my phone.

Instead of calling my uncle back, I redownload the Twitter app.

Maybe if I reread every single one of Owen Brodie's tweets with this new life-changing non-cynical perspective, I will find something funny in them and find something to like about him as a person.

But wait…

There's a message…

From Owen Brodie.

From a few days ago.

OWEN BRODIE: *That <winking face emoji> just confirmed that you think I'm hot. Thanks and have a nice day ;)*

Shit.

Shit shit shit.

There is literally nothing I can respond with that will make our forthcoming meeting any less awkward.

So I will ignore the message and delete the Twitter app again.

It's the only logical move I can make.

ME: *<face with rolling eyes emoji>*

Shit.

5

FRANKIE HOGAN JOKE
NOTEBOOK - JUNE

Anyone else hate being confused? Anyone like solid information based on actual facts that have been thoroughly researched by scientists? Here's a tip—never Google your questions about men.

I know you won't listen to me because I can tell how many girls and women are Googling questions like, "What does it mean if a guy says 'bless you' instead of 'Gesundheit' when you sneeze?" And then thirty online "articles" come up because those websites want more hits and they know that if they provide "answers" to these highly searched questions, they'll earn more ad revenue.

To be clear: I am not judging anyone in this terrible scenario—except maybe the guys who lead women to Google this idiotic stuff.

I read an online article that said 67% of men who use emojis in a text to a woman like like *that woman. 100%*

of twenty-six-year-old female comedians who Googled "What does it mean when a guy uses emojis with a woman?" are 50% certain that this is total horseshit. But the other 50% is like, really?! So he does like like *me?! OMG but what does it mean that he used an emoticon and not an emoji though?!*

100% of women who Google "What does it mean if he uses a winking emoticon instead of a winking face emoji?" were totally disappointed with the paltry number of outdated posts that attempted to explain the answer to this very important question.

100% of female roommates who try to convince you that if a grown man uses a winky emoticon instead of a winking face emoji that means he's flirting...are just messing with your head.

69% of women who laugh every time they see the number 69 are 96% more fun in bed than women who don't.

One out of infinity women don't really care if Owen Brodie is emoticon-flirting with her or not.

One out of one twenty-six-year-old female comedian who has a meeting set up with Owen Brodie and his young son is definitely not going to wear the crop top, jean shorts, and super cute wedge heels that her roommate recommended she wear to said meeting.

Zero percent of Frankie Hogans believe it matters that she woke up mid-orgasm from a dream where all Owen Brodie was doing was kissing her while gently massaging her hips—because she just had to pee. That's all it was. Shut up.

* 7 out of 10 of these might work in my stand-up act. The rest of them will never ever be thought of again. Especially the part about what a good kisser Owen Brodie was in my dream.

6

OWEN

I'm not saying I was hoping my manager's niece named Frankie would be @frankiesayrelax, but I'm not saying I'm disappointed to find a woman who looks an awful lot like @frankiesayrelax's profile picture standing at my doorstep in jean shorts either. She's also wearing a loose vintage *Star Wars* T-shirt and sneakers with no socks. They're probably meant to detract from the blatant white-hot sexiness of her short shorts, but they're failing miserably because her toned bare legs are slammin' and I need to stop imagining my head between them before my son joins us downstairs.

I could have let that face with rolling eyes emoji slide—because maybe she really does think I'm an asshat—but the basic guy-math equation that I'm solving in my head is: eye-roll emoji + jean shorts = This Chick Wants My Eggplant Emoji.

Unfortunately, the grown-up dad math equation goes something like this: If I hire her to be my kid's nanny + she's my manager's niece = I Can't Give It To Her.

Fuck.

"It's customary to greet an invited human who's standing on your doorstep with a few words of welcome before ushering her inside to meet your son —which is the only reason I'm here. To meet your son."

Such a little turd.

"You're my manager's niece." It's a statement, not a question.

"Yes. You're my uncle's client."

"Yes."

"Fancy that."

"Indeed. You're the Tampa heckler. From Twitter."

"The Tampa Heckler. Wow, I sound like a comic book villain… Small world."

"Absolutely fucking tiny. What's your last name again?"

I know what it is and you know I know what it is, but I'm gonna make you tell me anyway.

"Hogan. My last name is Hogan."

"Right. Not Hancock."

"Right."

"Interesting that Martin's office didn't give me your full name."

"It is interesting, isn't it."

She blows up at a few strands of hair that have fallen into her face and then carefully pushes them out of the way. Her long dark hair's pulled up into a ponytail, and *fucking hell,* I want to tug on that thing when her mouth is on my—*nope.*

Rein it in, Brodie.

She self-consciously touches the smooth skin of her bare neck and rocks back and forth the tiniest bit.

She's blushing.

I'm staring.

I should invite her in, but what's the point?

I can't hire this woman.

She clears her throat, shoves both hands into the front pockets of her jeans—which pushes her tits out more—and blurts out, "Okay, I'm just going to say it. The emojis didn't mean anything. Your emoticons didn't mean anything. My emojis meant nothing. Nobody was flirting with anyone. No one thinks anyone is hot. I'm wearing shorts because it's warm out. I need a job. Are you going to invite me in so I can meet your son, or should I just turn around and go home so you can stare at my ass while I walk away?"

"Well, you could just take it down a notch or twelve, missy."

She huffs. "You could just *not* call me missy." She

crosses her arms in front of her chest. "Seriously. Do you want me to leave or not?"

"All right. I mean, no. I don't want you to leave. Let's start over." I hold out my hand to shake hers. "Hi. I'm Owen Brodie. You must be Martin's niece, Frankie. Thanks for coming. Nice shorts."

She pulls her hand away and rolls her eyes at me.

"So when you roll your eyes at me in real life, that also doesn't mean anything, correct?

"Correct."

"Got it. Please come in." I stand aside, pushing the front door open more with my back, but not so far that she doesn't have to brush the side of her arm against my chest when she passes by.

She gives me the side-eye as she crosses the threshold, probably watching to see if I check out her ass.

What am I? A drunk twenty-year-old frat boy? I'm a thirty-year-old formerly married man who has fathered a child and owns a house. I know how to perform undetected ass-checks.

Somebody needs to get over herself.

But when she stops in the middle of the foyer to look around, I have to say—she does have a great ass.

"Nice house."

"Thanks."

"I don't come to Santa Monica much. This seems like a really nice, quiet neighborhood."

"It is. Why do you sound so surprised?"

"I don't know. I guess I just pictured you living in a penthouse on the Sunset Strip, behind a billboard of yourself selling overpriced watches or men's chest lotion or something."

"That's not a thing. There's no lotion that's made specifically for men's chests—I know because I've searched for it online. Multiple times."

"Well, if there were, I'm sure the company would hire you to be their shill."

"Thank you."

"I mean, that wasn't a compliment, but—"

"It was. Thank you."

Another eye-roll with an accompanying head shake.

What a treat!

"Would you like to have a seat in the living room, milady?"

"Sure. Is your son actually here? Sam, right?"

"Yes. He's upstairs, watching something on his iPad or sleeping. I thought I'd ask you a few questions first."

"Okie dokie."

I lead her to the living room. This house isn't big but it's classy as fuck, and I can see by the way she's eyeing my very tasteful décor that she's impressed and I can see that it kills her to be impressed by anything me-related. And I fucking love it.

I take a seat in the vintage Herman Miller lounge chair—the one that cost seven thousand dollars. The one that makes me feel like a boss every time I sit in it. The one with the rosewood back that Sam carved his name into. I wasn't even mad at him because one day this will be his and good for him for staking his claim. Big Daddy's got his back, and he's going to do what's best for both of us by *not* hiring this snarky vixen.

I wait for her to remove her shoulder bag, place it on the floor next to her feet, and take a seat on the sofa. She sits with her thighs squeezed together. Possibly because she doesn't want me to see up her shorts, but more likely because there's a lot of tension between those legs, courtesy of yours truly. And it's going to get so much worse.

She finally stops fidgeting and looks me in the eyes, almost daring me to question her.

"So you're from Tampa?"

"Yes. The city of gators and your in-laws."

"Former in-laws. How long have you been out here?"

"About two years."

"Uh-huh. And you're doing stand-up? Why haven't I seen you around the circuit?"

"We aren't exactly in the same circuit, are we?"

"You could still go to shows."

"I do go to shows. Just not yours."

"Which begs the question—why did you agree to interview for this job?"

"I told you. I need a job. So I'm here to meet your

son and determine if I can put up with you for a month or whatever."

"I see. You're here to interview *me*."

"Well, that makes it sound like I'm here to write an article about you or something. If I were going to interview comedians, there are approximately five thousand I would want to talk to before you."

"Save the best for last, you mean."

I watch her struggle with her facial muscles, trying so hard not to smile at that. "No. That's not what I mean. Are you sure you wouldn't like to ask me more child caregiver-related questions?"

"Are you twenty-five or older?"

"I'm one year older than twenty-five. Why?"

"Because Sam's nanny would have to drive a rental car at some point while we're out of town. One must be at least twenty-five years of age to rent a car in this country."

"Well, I am of car-renting age and I also have a perfectly clean driving record."

"Uh-huh. I'll need proof of that. Marty said you have a lot of experience with looking after kids, but he didn't clarify."

"Don't call him Marty. And yes. I do. In Tampa and when I was in college. I actually got certified from the Red Cross when I was in high school."

"For what? Joke and tweet assessment?"

She almost laughs at that, and it feels fucking great.

"For babysitting and advanced child care. First aid and CPR."

Shit.

She's trained for this.

"Cool. I didn't know that was a thing."

"Well, you were probably too busy being a model to babysit when you were in high school."

"Damn right I was. Paid for my entire college education."

"I bet. And this house, I suppose?"

"The down payment, sure."

"Are you still modeling at all?"

"Only if I get an offer I can't refuse. I'm a full-time comedian now. As you know, I have a cute family comedy series in development."

She rubs her glossy lips together and frowns. I've annoyed her by reminding her of her adorable drunk messages. Oops.

"I did notice the headline in the trades, yes," she says through clenched teeth. "Congratulations. I'm glad they got Shane Miller to direct the pilot. He's awesome. And funny." She smirks at me. "And he has great hair."

How dare you.

I stare her down, giving her my most intense model-gaze, while combing my fingers through my hair. Because Shane Miller *is* awesome and funny, and yeah, he might even have great hair—but no man has better hair than I do.

She just stares back, blinking slowly. "Why don't you tell me a little bit about your son. Do you share custody of him with his mother? If you don't mind my asking."

I rub the back of my neck, drawing attention to my unbearably sleek jawline. "Yes, we share custody, fifty-fifty, usually. But my ex-wife and her new husband just had a baby." I lower my voice a little. "I don't think Sam's getting enough attention when he's at their place, so I didn't want to leave him for an entire month while I'm on tour."

Her eyes soften a little, along with her voice and posture and her entire being, maybe even. "That's nice. I'm sure he'll appreciate that."

"Yeah, well. That's the thing about Sam. I'm sure he will appreciate it, but he's a bit…stoic. He's a great kid, but he's super chill. He likes to take naps. He probably will for the rest of his life, I don't know. Ashley kept taking him to the doctor to see if there's something wrong with his thyroid, and she had him talk to a child psychologist once to see if he's depressed. But he just likes to take naps."

"I would literally nap all day if I could."

"Well then, maybe you should have your thyroid checked out."

She doesn't roll her eyes. She just looks at me like that flat line for a mouth emoji.

"Anyway, he's really smart and cool and responsible and low key and serious. So if you meet him, don't be offended if you don't see much of a response. That's just what he's like."

"*If* I meet him?"

I smile and blink at her, saying nothing.

She crosses her slammin' legs, grasps one knee with both hands, and stares at me for a beat before saying, "So…does Sam have any allergies?"

"He's allergic to sass and sarcasm, so I don't think this is going to work out."

"Yeah, well, my eyeballs are allergic to your face, so I agree this is a bad idea." She stands up.

"Thanks for stopping by. I'll tell Martin you're overqualified for the job."

She picks up her shoulder bag like she's mad at it. "Great. I'll tell him I'd rather clean sewers than spend a month on the road with you." Her eyes are watery. Her lower lip is quivering.

Shit.

I'm an asshole.

But so is she.

So maybe she's perfectly qualified for this job.

I get up and cross over to her. "Listen, I…" I start to reach out to her, to console her because I want to make her feel better. There's a vulnerability just beneath the surface that I can see so clearly. I recognize it, and I want to make her feel good and better about *everything*—which is weird. But I stop when I follow her gaze and see that Sam is standing in the entrance to the living room.

"Hey, buddy. I didn't hear you come downstairs."

"Yeah." He gives Frankie a perfunctory wave. "Hey."

"Heyyyy, Sam. Sup?"

"Hey."

"Sam, this is Frankie. She was just—"

"Hi, Frankie. I like your T-shirt."

"Oh, thanks. You a Star Wars fan?"

"Yeah. The old stuff."

"Me too. I mean, I like Rey and Kylo though."

"Me too! I want to go as Kylo for Halloween this year."

This is already the most he's ever said to a total stranger, which is disturbing.

"Awesome!"

He shrugs. "My dad thinks we should go as Han Solo and Chewbacca."

"Well, that would only work if *you're* Han Solo and he's Chewbacca."

"I know, that's what I said. But he doesn't want to cover up his face."

She shakes her head. "Sounds about right."

"Are you leaving?"

"Well, I've been having a terrible time talking to your dad over here, so I was about to run out."

Sam laughs.

Laughs.

Just to be polite, I'm sure.

"Yeah, he's pretty bad."

"Yeah, he's the worst, I'd say. So what were you watching up there?"

Sam scratches his nose with the back of his hand and walks over to be closer to her.

Which is unusual.

And unfortunate.

She sits back down on the sofa and pats the cushion next to her, gesturing for him to join her there.

And he does.

Which is really fucking weird.

She gives me a look, like maybe I should take a step back so they can bond.

Which I don't want them to do.

But Sam looks so happy.

And comfortable.

So I go back to my Herman Miller chair and wait for my son to realize what a cheeky little turd this lady is.

He will.

I have faith in him.

7

FRANKIE

I have never been so aroused and angered by a man while talking to a child before.

How do married people do this?

There's no way I can do this for a month.

Owen Brodie is infuriating and full of himself, and he's wearing glasses today, which makes him look more down-to-earth and approachable—which just makes me even angrier for some reason. I want to punch him in the face, but I know better than to punch someone when they're wearing glasses. And judging by his biceps, he could probably punch me back pretty good—and I wouldn't put it past him to try it either. So I will restrain myself.

His ex-wife must be a wonderful person because this kid is great and I see very little resemblance to his father aside from the electric-blue eyes and a little cleft chin that will probably cause a lot of trouble for girls in about ten years.

Not that it's the electric-blue eyes or the dimple in Owen Brodie's chin that's causing trouble for me.

It's the entire fucking package.

But this is about Sam Brodie, so I need to focus on him.

He shrugs in response to my question about what he was watching upstairs. "Nature show. Nobody died in it though, so it was kind of boring, I guess."

"I mean, what's the point, right? Have you seen the one where the shark jumps out of the water and eats the seal?"

His face lights up like I just asked him if he's ever met Santa Claus. "Yeah! That was so awesome."

"I felt really bad for the seal, but it was a cool shot."

I can sense his father cringing over there, but I'm not going to look at him.

Sam nods enthusiastically. "Yeah, me too. But I like that kind of stuff because sometimes, when I don't like stuff in my life, I think about how at least I'm not being eaten by a shark." He shrugs again. "And then I feel better."

"You are a wise man."

Owen clears his throat. "Your life's pretty great though. Huh, buddy?"

"It's fine. But sometimes really dumb kids in my

class get better grades than I do, even though I'm smarter than they are. It's annoying."

This kid is really speaking my language.

And *now* I look up at his dad when I say, "Yes. It is annoying when other people do really well, even though you're more awesome than they are. But that's life. And eventually everyone will realize how smart you are. Right, Mr. Brodie?"

Wow, his jaw is clenched so tight. I hope he doesn't hurt his face.

"Sam actually gets really good grades, and it's important for everyone to have a positive attitude and to not compare themselves to other people. Right, Sam?"

"Tell that to the seal," Sam and I both say at the same time.

I hold my hand up for Sam to high-five me, and he almost doubles over from laughing so hard.

Owen watches in dismay.

I guess his son has never laughed at *him* this much, or something.

I guess I should feel bad for Owen.

But I feel really, really great about myself.

"We're funny," I say to Sam conspiratorially. Like it's *our* thing.

"Yeah. We are."

"I'm sure the seal went around thinking he was funnier and more awesome than everyone else too... until he got eaten alive," Owen mutters.

Sam and I both turn to stare at him.

He frowns at me defiantly.

"Well. That escalated quickly."

"I just want to be clear that that's not going to happen to you, Sam," he says reassuringly. "You're not going to get eaten alive by anything."

"Ohhh-kayyy."

I give Sam a little nudge. "That's comforting, huh?"

"I'm just saying—"

"So, Sam." I talk over Owen and try to change the subject. "I hear you're going on a big trip with your dad. You excited?"

"Sometimes. I'm excited to see my uncle in New York. He says the pizza there is better than here."

"Oh, it is, for sure. The crust is really thin, so you can fold it up and eat it while you're walking around."

"Hmmm. I like to sit or lie down when I'm eating though."

"Well, you can do that too. But people walk around a lot in New York, is the thing. So sometimes you have to eat while you're on the go."

"Oh. Hmm." He touches the tip of his finger to his chin. "I hope I don't have to walk around a lot."

"Don't worry about it, buddy," Owen chimes in. "She doesn't know what we'll be up to in New York. We can do whatever you want. Plus, we're going to lots of other fun cities. Like

Tampa." He gives me a look. "Remember Tampa?"

Sam wrinkles his nose. "Where Grandma and Grandpa live?"

"Yeah."

"I didn't like it there."

"Yeah, me neither."

Sam turns to me. "But you're coming on the trip with us, right?"

"Oh, I don't know. I might be busy, and I think your dad has to meet with some other people." I stand up slowly. "I should get going actually."

"I like *you* though."

"Well, I like you too, Sam. But you should probably meet the other people too."

"We already met five other ladies, and I didn't like talking to any of them." He turns to his dad again. "Dad. Tell her she can come with us."

Owen stands up too. "We need to let Frankie go so she can check her schedule, okay?"

"Can't you check it on your phone?" he asks me.

Smart kid.

Great taste too.

But he comes with a dad that I do not have a taste for.

"I really do have to get going now, Sam," I say firmly but kindly. "It was so nice to meet you." I hold my hand out to shake his.

He pouts but shakes my hand and then crosses

his arms in front of his chest and frowns at the floor in front of him.

"Hopefully I'll see you again," I say to him, picking up my bag and starting for the front door.

"You want to walk Frankie to the door, Sam?"

"No."

"Fair enough."

I try to get out of this house before Owen can catch up with me, but that fucker is fast. You'd think the upright hair would slow him down, but the sleek jawline probably helps him to glide through the air like a sarcasm-seeking missile.

He unlocks and opens the door, staring down at me. "Thanks for coming by."

"He's a great kid."

"I know." He gestures for me to step outside and then follows me, lowering his voice. "Look, obviously Sam liked you, but it's also pretty obvious it wouldn't be a good idea for..." He waves back and forth between us.

I would love for him to finish that sentence with words, but it doesn't seem like he's planning to.

"I agree. He did like me. And no, it wouldn't." I turn to walk the path to the front gate. "See you around, Owen Brodie."

I don't look over my shoulder to see if he's checking out my ass because I can actually feel his eyes on me.

He hasn't moved.

Hasn't turned away from me.

But he's letting me leave.

And I'd better go home to practice carrying dishes of food while I walk, smiling at strangers who want me to bring them things, and being around food without eating it.

On a positive note—since I have such a great new attitude—I'll have a lot of new material for my stand-up act.

8

TO: frankieisfunny7@gmail.com
FROM: owenbrodieishilarious@gmail.com

Dear Ms. Hogan,

I'm emailing to offer you the job as my son's nanny because Sam had a temper tantrum when I told him I can't hire you to come on my stand-up tour with us. "She heckled me at a club a few years ago," I wanted to say. "She is the sassy little turd who trolls me on Twitter," I could have told him. "She's an even bigger pain in the butt when we're face-to-face," I thought to myself. What I would never tell him is—*things could get complicated. For reasons.*

Let me know if you want the job.

With great reluctance,
Owen

#AdorableHowObsessedYouAreWithMe

P.S. Were there six Frankies before you who also think they're funny?

TO: owenbrodieishilarious@gmail.com
FROM: frankieisfunny7@gmail.com

Dear Mr. Brodie,

Thank you for your email. Please inform Sam that I like him very much and would love to be his nanny and accompany him on your terrible joke of a stand-up tour.

I can assure you—things will not get complicated. For many, many reasons.

Primarily because Owen Brodie isn't funny, and he can suck it.

Out of financial desperation and a fondness for your son,
Frankie

#GetOverYourselfPrettyBoy

P.S. There were only five funny Frankies before me. Gmail suggested frankieisfunny6 for my username at first so I used that for a while. But my mother is Australian and when most Australians say the word "sex" it sounds like "six." So when my mum told Australians my email address they thought she said "frankieisfunnysex." So I wouldn't get their emails. And I'm not funny sex. So I changed it to 7.

P.P.S. I guess the only time anyone has ever written the words "Owen Brodie is hilarious" is when they email you.
Clever.
And sad.

TO: Frankie Hogan
FROM: Owen Brodie

Actually, I created this Gmail account just for you, so YOU would have to type out the words "Owen Brodie is hilarious." Pretty hilarious, huh?

I'm glad you've agreed to be Sam's nanny. For his sake. I'll have my business manager send you some paperwork and get your payment info. I'm sure Martin told you that we'll need you with us for one month. In addition to your weekly salary, I will be paying for your travel, hotel accommodations, and meals. If you need any money to cover incidentals, just let me know.

I'm attaching the itinerary for my tour. We're flying to the East Coast first and working our way back west. As I mentioned earlier, we're going to Tampa, so if you still have family there, you can see them because Sam will be spending the night with his mother's parents.

I should warn you that since I'll be doing shows at theaters instead of over-twenty-one comedy clubs, I will be asking you to accompany my son to my shows on occasion. At least until his bedtime. But I will literally be paying you to hear me perform, so I guess the joke's on me because I can't stop you from heckling me.

TO: Owen Brodie
FROM: Frankie Hogan

I guess you aren't very clever after all, Mr. Brodie, since I didn't have to type out your email address. I just hit Reply to your email.

TO: Frankie Hogan
FROM: Owen Brodie

Copy-pasted from your email: P.P.S. I guess the only time anyone has ever written the words "Owen Brodie is hilarious" is when they email you. Clever.

Yes. It was clever.

Please give me your phone number for non-flirtational Sam-related purposes only.
Mine is (310) 555-9765

TO: Owen Brodie
FROM: Frankie Hogan

(813) 555-3697

Are we going to schedule a time for me to get to know Sam a little better before we actually go on tour? Obviously he already likes me, but I want to make sure he's comfortable with me before we travel together.

TO: Frankie Hogan
FROM: Owen Brodie

Yes.

Have you really dated nine guys named Justin?

TO: Owen Brodie
FROM: Frankie Hogan

Oh my God stop watching my YouTube videos!!!!!!

TO: Frankie Hogan
FROM: Owen Brodie

No.

9

FRANKIE HOGAN'S YOUTUBE VIDEO

(Which Owen Brodie Can't Stop Watching)

"I love my parents. They're so sweet. My mother's from Australia, and my dad's a Kentucky boy who moved to Florida, so when I was a little kid in Tampa, I was very confused about how to speak English. Apparently when I first started going to daycare, I was like, 'Butter my butt and call me a biscuit! I'm *stahvin'*! Can I get a chokkie biccy after I go to the *torlet*? Fair dinkum, y'all!'

"Can't say that I've gotten any less confused about how to speak English, but I've gotten a lot better at hiding my confusion. This is true about absolutely everything in life, by the way. I have literally no idea how to live like an adult most of the time, but I've gotten really good at acting like I know everything.

"My mother, on the other hand, knows exactly everything about how I should be doing things. Like for my stand-up act, for instance. I don't know if people who grow up to be brain surgeons or astronauts always have people saying to them, 'Oh, you know what you should do when you're operating on someone's brain? You should use toothpicks!' Or 'I had this hilarious thing happen to me the other day, and you should use it the next time you go to the moon!'

"But when you're a stand-up comic, you get a lot of people telling you about all the funny things you should be talking about in your act, and my mum has sent me approximately nine thousand emails filled with what she considers to be joke material. So I thought I'd share a small sample of some of my notes on her suggestions with you…"

Frankie pulls a little notebook out from her back pocket, opens it up, clears her throat, and starts speaking in her mother's Australian accent.

"Y'know how when ya go to *Stahbucks* to order coffee and they ask for your name to write on the cup? What if you told them your name was You Arsehole? Then when your order is up they'd have to call out, 'Grande Blonde Vanilla Latte for You Arsehole!'

"How about a bit about laundry baskets? Y'know

how no matter how big your laundry basket is, it always fills up faster than you can do the wash? Why can't my bank account keep refilling as fast as my laundry basket? Why is it that the laundry basket suddenly gets filled up again every time I ask your dad to fold his laundry and put it away? What did people used to use chairs for in their bedrooms before there were clothes that aren't dirty enough for the laundry basket and not clean enough for the closet?"

She doesn't get the laughs that she deserves from that bit, so she closes the notebook and returns it to her back pocket.

She places the mic on the stand and picks up the ukulele from the stool next to her.

"Speaking of laundry, did any women here have a real orgasm while they were in high school? Can I see a show of hands?...You, ma'am? And was it that hand that gave you the orgasm or another person?... Yeah, that's what I thought. I too experienced exactly no orgasms while making out with guys in high school, but when I was seventeen, I had a boyfriend who was very sweet. We'll call him Justin. Because that was his name. He was my third Justin. This is a little song I wrote about Justin Number Three."

She strums the ukulele a few times and then puts it down when she sings like Taylor Swift—sort of.

"I'm so glad you tried so hard to make me

Feel good with your fingers while you kissed me
Most guys just squeezed my boobs, but you—
You always tried to do that thing
I'm just not sure what you were trying for...
But I appreciate the effort

Because you almost made come once
And I remember how every time you jizzed your pants
You asked, 'Did you come?'
And I was like, 'I think so!'
But I didn't
But I'm still grateful anyway."

She strums the ukulele again.

"That's it. That's the whole song. I'm Frankie Hogan—thank you so much."

OWEN

I need to stop thinking about Frankie fucking Hogan so I can concentrate on this Zoom meeting.

She's downstairs with Sam. They're watching her DVD of *Crocodile Dundee*—which is PG-13, and I'm not sure that he should be watching it—but I can hear them laughing. Both of them. Sam…is laughing. With Frankie fucking Hogan. When I put on *Gremlins* last night, he just fell asleep.

"Uh, Brodie?"

I snap out of it and look back up at my monitor, at Shane Miller's adorable smirking face.

"I can't tell if you're angry or aroused right now, buddy."

"Neither. I'm formulating my thoughts on whatever thing whichever one of you said just now."

The producer of my show, Barry Weiner, was once the producer of *That's So Wizard*—the Disney

Channel series that launched the illustrious careers of such talents as Shane Miller, Nico Todd, Alex Vega, and my asshole little brother. Barry's produced numerous other hit shows for that network as well as several critically acclaimed independent films, including the one that Alex directed and Shane starred in. So what is he doing producing this piece of crap thing that I'm somehow getting paid a shit ton of money to star in? What are any of us doing here?

We're discussing the first draft of the pilot script for *Untitled Owen Brodie Family Comedy Project*. That's how well-defined the show is now—we don't even have an actual title. I didn't hate the script. It's fine. The writer's good, but he's not in this meeting. I mean, it's a lighthearted family sitcom about a single dad stand-up comic and his three little kids who don't think he's funny. There are some really good fart jokes, a few cute moments between the father and his kids, and it took me an hour and a half to read twenty-five pages because I kept watching Frankie's YouTube videos and checking to see if her Twitter account was back up.

"I think that on a live action family sitcom scale of one to ten," Barry says, "where anything that I didn't produce is a one, and *That's So Wizard* is a ten, this draft of this script is a five. If we can get the next draft to a seven by next week, we're golden. How do we do that without hiring another writer? Because I can't bring in a writing staff until episode two."

"What if my character needs to hire a nanny for his kids?" I find myself blurting out.

"Go on…" Shane says, like he's my shrink.

"And you know how his kids don't think he's funny? What if this woman he hires is sort of a sassy, struggling stand-up comic herself? And she doesn't think I'm funny. Like, she heckles me during my opening stand-up bit in the pilot. But she ends up becoming the nanny, and my kids think she's hilarious. And obviously she's a love interest, but they sort of hate each other so there's a lot of sexual tension. And then there's this other layer of conflict because my kids just think she's cooler than me. Is that something? Or is that too much like *The Nanny?*"

"Well, it's not too much like *The Nanny* because the show isn't centered around the nanny and also you're both comedians. Your character isn't British, and hers isn't from Queens. And they've already picked us up for an entire season, so who gives a shit. But the addition of a nanny character is good. I mean, we aren't allowed to use terms like 'sexual tension' in the world of family sitcom development," Barry informs me, "but I like that idea a lot. Especially if we can get a bangin' hot chick for the nanny."

"Are we allowed to use the term 'bangin' hot chick' in the world of family sitcom development?"

"I think what makes that work," Shane offers before Barry can start listing all the hot young actresses he'd like to bang, "is that it gives us the opportunity to create a slightly bigger family type situation for you guys. All TV shows are about family dynamics, right? This way we have a potential mother-slash-wife figure."

"Is she though? Does she have that kind of potential? To be a mother-slash-wife figure? While she's employed as the nanny?"

"I mean, she has to, or what's the point?" Barry says. "Especially if she's hot."

"Well, she *is* hot. I mean, she would be. But she's also kind of a little turd to me. To him. My character."

"Well, they always are," Shane says, smirking.

"Right." Barry claps his hands together once, definitively, startling me. "This character addition gets us to seven out of ten by the next draft. Maybe even an eight. Then we can get the script to the executives, get their notes, and then hire a staff and bang out the rest of the season. Good talk, you guys. We all happy? We good?"

"Yeah, we're good. Good talk."

"You'll have a cast list for the nanny by tomorrow, I'm guessing. Right, Barry?" Shane asks.

"Ohhh, you know it. Talk soon." Barry leaves the meeting.

"You have time to talk for another minute?" Shane asks me.

"Yeah." Things have gone quiet downstairs. I wonder if Sam fell asleep. "What's up?"

He leans forward, closer to his laptop camera. "You tell me. Did you hire a new nanny or something?"

I turn the volume down on my laptop and lower my voice. My bedroom door's closed, but I definitely don't want Frankie fucking Hogan to hear this. "What? Yeah. Yes. I did. Just for the tour. Why?"

"She's a hot little turd, huh?"

I do my best Barry Weiner imitation. "Ohhh, you know it." I have no idea what my face is doing, but apparently Shane Miller knows exactly what it's saying.

"Been there."

"You have? Wait. What?" Now I'm confused. "You mean Scary Nanny?"

"No. My wife. Willa. She was the nanny for a little while. You didn't know that?"

"No. I thought she was a perfumer."

"Well, she is a perfumer. She was then too. But I needed a temp nanny when my ex-wife was out of town. Has Ashley met her yet?"

"Yeah, they met for coffee yesterday, and Ashley approved of her, which was...surprising. I mean, Sam loves her, which is annoying. My manager obviously likes her—he's her uncle. Apparently everyone in my life likes her. Which is troubling."

"She's Martin's niece? You need to talk to him first before you make any moves."

"I'm not making any moves. There are no moves to be made. Not while she's the nanny. Wait—can I make moves while she's the nanny?"

"It's not ideal… Hang on." He looks offscreen to talk to someone. "Summer, I'm not finished with my Zoom meeting yet."

I can hear his daughter Summer ask, "Who are you talking to? Is it Zac Efron?"

"No. It's never Zac Efron. It's Owen Brodie. He's Dylan's brother, remember?"

Suddenly, Shane's little girl's smiling face appears in the Zoom window. "Heyyy, Owen. Remember me?" She does a little hair toss. Such a little flirt.

"Of course I remember you. Hey, Summer. You're the one who taught Sam about pocket snacks. I did the laundry yesterday and found melted cheese in the pocket of his pants, so that was awesome."

"Oh, I don't do pocket snacks anymore," she states, waving her hand dismissively. "That's for little kids."

Shane looks down, reaches into the front pocket of her pants, and then holds up a few pretzel sticks.

Summer smacks her lips together, blushing. "Heyyy, how'd they get in there?"

"I'll let you go," Shane says. "But to sum up—talk

to your manager before you do anything serious, and also Willa wanted me to ask you if you can comp her grammie for your Detroit show. Apparently Grammie Todd is a big fan of yours."

I would really love to ask him what exactly counts as something serious where nannies are concerned. Like, are we talking anything beyond finger banging? Marriage proposals? Or butt-stuff negotiations? But I also can't think about fingers, butts, or sex at all now that Grammie Todd is in my head. "Yeah, Nico already mentioned that actually. She's on the list."

"I wanna be on the list!" Summer yells out.

"Right on. Talk soon." Shane exits the meeting just as Summer's face gets closer to the camera.

I can't talk to my manager about his niece. I mean, there's nothing to talk about. But what would I say if there were? *"Hi, can you make sure all the water they provide for me at the venues are filtered and room temperature, and also I'm planning on throwing a couple of winky-face emojis your niece's way and then punishing her for heckling me by giving her the ol' tongue plow until she weeps and declares me the king of her pussy. Then I'll fuck her in all the ways a man can fuck a woman because she'll be begging for it. All of that will take place within a period of about half an hour, probably while my son is taking a nap. Is that cool with you?"*

When I get downstairs, I peer into the living room. The movie is still on, but Sam is curled up on the sofa, fast asleep. Frankie isn't in here, but I hear movement in the kitchen. She's washing the dishes that were in the sink. I actually put my hand over my heart because it feels warm and filled with longing all of a sudden.

I have this sudden flashback of being a little kid, in the family room with my brothers. The TV on, volume low because my dad's reading a book in his chair, and my mom's in the kitchen.

I never had that feeling of comfort, that sense of being home when it was Sam and Ashley and me.

I don't know why I'm feeling it now. Maybe I'm hungry. Literally hungry. Maybe I need a snack. Or maybe it's because Frankie is the first woman to be alone with Sam and me in this house—besides my ex-wife, Nanny Blanca, my housekeeper, or Mrs. Billings.

More specifically, she's the first woman to be alone with Sam and me in this house who I've jerked it to. Angrily. Repeatedly. To great satisfaction.

Against my better judgment, I join her in the kitchen. She's singing to herself, very quietly, bobbing her head, swaying her shoulders and hips the tiniest bit. All sexy-like. But cute. Lost in the song and the feeling. I know the song, and I know the feeling.

It's creepy that I'm standing here, leaning against the doorframe, watching her.

But if she doesn't want me to watch her quietly

sing and dance while washing my dishes, then maybe she shouldn't do it in my house when she knows I'm here.

"I like that song," I say in a hushed voice after she's put down the glass she was drying with a dish towel.

She freezes, stops singing.

"You like Led Zeppelin?"

"Yes." She's still not moving. Head tilted just a bit in my direction. Tense.

I walk over to the cupboards near where she's standing by the sink, open one to take out a glass.

She wipes her hands on the front of her jeans—no shorts today—and steps away from me.

"Thank you for doing the dishes. Can I get you anything? You hungry?"

She's now standing in front of the water dispenser. I walk over there with my glass. She steps aside again.

"Nope. We had a snack. He fell asleep. You probably saw."

"Yeah. Sounds like he was enjoying the show before that though."

She smiles. "He really did. I'll leave the DVD here so you can finish watching it with him later."

"You leaving?"

"Oh. Did you want me to stay? I can if you want me to."

"Up to you."

She nods. "I guess I should get going, then."

"Okay. How was your meeting with Ashley? She said it was great."

"Yeah." She crosses her arms in front of her chest, crosses one leg in front of the other. "She's nice."

"Was she?"

"Her baby's so cute."

"Yeah."

"Do you get along with her new husband?"

"Yeah, he's fine. We don't hang out or anything." I gulp down the glass of water, place the empty glass in the sink. I think I'll put away the dishes from the dishwasher. See if she stays to help. I glance over at her, super casually, as I open the dishwasher door.

She seems so anxious. "Why are you looking at me like that?"

"I'm not. Your hair is different."

"Different from what?"

"From the last time you were here. And from your profile pic. And from your YouTube videos."

She pushes a few loose strands of hair behind an ear. "I can't tell if you're being serious or not."

"It looks good. You look pretty."

"Thank you. I feel very uncomfortable."

"You're welcome. So, *have* you really dated nine guys named Justin?"

She shakes her head and rubs her forehead, laughing. "Oh my God. Did you really watch my YouTube videos? All of them?"

"Just answer the question."

When I put away the first of the dishes, she goes over to the dishwasher to pull out the dishes and hand them to me. Helping me, without me even having to ask. I like that.

"You answer mine first," she insists.

"You already know I did."

"How many times?

"Okay, maybe you should get over yourself too. I had to do some background research to make sure my son's nanny isn't psychotic. Or a terrible comedian."

"And what was your conclusion based on my YouTube videos?"

"You're definitely funny. I like your act. You're funny. You're really funny. And talented. Why are you looking at me like that?"

"I'm not."

"You are. You look like you're going to cry."

"I'm not."

"Anyway."

"No, just… Let me just… Give me a minute to actually experience this."

Now *I'm* rolling my eyes.

She takes a deep breath and then looks me straight in the eye and says, "Thank you."

"Okay."

"No really. Thank you. For saying that and for watching the videos. No matter how many times."

"It wasn't that many."

"If you say so. But thank you."

"You're welcome."

I close the door to a cupboard, and we just stand where we are for a few seconds.

"This feels weird," she finally says.

"It really does… So—nine Justins?"

She laughs and pulls out the silverware basket and hands it to me. It has literally never occurred to me to do that when emptying out the dishwasher. Fascinating.

"Yes. But I didn't exactly date the first two. I was, like, fifteen, but you know. They *like* liked me. I had crushes on them before we were going out, so it was a big deal." She suddenly gives me a very intense, angry look. "Not that anything means anything when you're that young. I mean, I don't even remember what they looked like, really."

"You don't?"

"No. It was ages ago."

She is very defensive all a sudden.

"I bet one hundred percent of your exes wear hoodies."

"What is that supposed to mean?" She seems so offended.

"I'm right, aren't I?"

"That's none of your business."

"You're right." We've been speaking quietly, so as not to wake up Sam, but I lower my voice even more. "Well I guess if we're sticking to what *is* my business, I will say that I'd prefer it if you don't have any male companions in your hotel rooms while we're traveling with Sam."

"Uh. Okay. Are you going to have female companions in your room?"

"No. Sam will be staying in my room."

"Oh. Right. But what about, like, for dates. Like after your shows or whatever. I'm going to be staying in your room while Sam sleeps?"

"Yes, you'll be staying in my room while Sam sleeps, while I'm doing my shows. But I don't plan to bed women while I'm on the road with my son. I might hang out with friends or other comics for a little while after the shows. Do you have a problem with that?"

"No. Of course you're going to do that. I mean, I have a tiny problem with the term *to bed women*, but I'm guessing you only said that to annoy me."

"Did it work?"

"Everything you say works, if your goal is to annoy me."

"Are you staying off Twitter because of me?"

She both smirks and blushes at the same time—which is amazing. "How do you know I'm off Twitter?"

"You need to be on Twitter. What if someone wants to book you? You don't have an agent, right?"

"Correct. And I reactivated my account this morning."

"Oh. Good."

"And if someone wanted to book me, I guess I wouldn't be available for a month anyway."

"Actually, I'll have a few nights off. You could find an open mic. Out-of-town shows are always great for trying out new material."

"Right." Now she's just straight-up smirking at me. "Like what you dazzled us with in Tampa that time."

I give her a look. "Left an impression on you though, didn't I?"

"You have to stop looking at me like that."

"Like what?"

"Hot Guy Look."

"I'm a hot guy. I can't *not* do this."

"You're definitely doing a thing, and you can't refer to yourself as a hot guy! That's just wrong."

"If looking hot is wrong, then I don't wanna be right."

"Okay. Well, I'm going to leave now. Hopefully Sam won't be upset that I'm not here when he wakes up."

"You want to stay for dinner?" I find myself saying. Which is weird. "Not like a date." Which just made it weirder. "Just as the nanny." Which just confirmed to both of us that I am, in fact, creepy.

She rubs her glossy lips together, eyes wide,

stares at me for a few seconds. It feels like she might actually say yes. Because it really feels like she shouldn't leave yet.

"I need to go home and do laundry and start packing."

"Right."

"For the trip."

"Sure."

"That I'm going on as your nanny."

"Exactly."

"I know it's a little early to start packing, but I don't like to leave things to the last minute."

"Smart. Thanks for hanging out with Sam today."

"Yeah, he's great. Thanks for having me... I'll let myself out."

"I'll just keep standing right here."

We stare at each other for another two or three or infinity seconds.

"Okay, bye."

And she's gone.

"And she took all the sunshine with her," I mutter to myself. "Lady Hilarious McFunnyPants, ladies and gentlemen."

FRANKIE HOGAN JOKE
NOTEBOOK - JULY

Here's something that isn't funny at all and will never ever find its way into my act or an actual conversation with another human or back into my brain again. Ever. I'm just going to let myself think about it now. Once. And then I will forget about it. Again.

Or maybe I'll write a short story about it and submit it to some online lady porn magazine—that's a thing, right? Under a pen name. Hoagie Frankin, perhaps.

A sweet, funny, annoying, eventually erotic little wisp of a story about a fourteen-year-old girl whose childhood best friend had just moved to another state and her other friends had suddenly grown massive boobs over the summer so they weren't nice to her anymore, and she was so lonely. To make matters worse, she had seen pictures of Kristen Stewart with kind of short, messy black hair and begged her mum, who's a hair stylist, to make her look exactly like that. Her mum cut her hair exactly like the picture, and yet she did not look like that. At all. Because, as her mother told her, her hair shafts are too thick and smooth, so they just want to hang straight. She looked like Keanu Reeves, and this was unacceptable.

So she went back to her mum's hair salon and asked her to cut it again, a different style. If she was going to look like a boy, she wanted to look like Taylor Lautner. With hair that stood up. While she waited for her mum to finish up with a client, she looked through the magazines in the waiting area. And there was this one ad in this one magazine of this one guy. She'd never seen a guy who was that handsome before. Pretty, even. He must have been a few years older than her, but the way he was looking at the camera, with those electric-blue eyes, it was like he was staring deep into her soul. She felt seen. She felt pretty. She felt adored.

She tore that page from the magazine.

She flipped through every other magazine in the pile, looking for more ads with more pictures of that guy, but she didn't find any.

She told her mum she didn't need a haircut anymore and went to the nearest drugstore to calmly peruse the magazine section and then used her babysitting money to purchase two teen magazines that featured ads and spreads of this pretty, handsome guy who was not quite a boy, not yet a man. Hot dog, he was hot. He was so much hotter than Justin P. and maybe even hotter than Justin H.

She carefully tore the images of this boy-man from the magazines and then carefully taped them up on the wall *of her bedroom. He was the only Person of Penis on the walls of her bedroom. But he looked right at home there, with Taylor Swift and Rhianna and Kelly Clarkson (this was before she had gotten into comedy and put up pictures of comedians).*

She didn't know his name, but she felt some kind of connection to him nevertheless. It may have been the loneliness. It may have been the hormones. Or maybe. Just maybe. She was destined to meet him one day.

Then one night she was watching something on TV— doesn't matter what—okay fine, it was Glee. *And she saw a commercial for Levi's jeans, and there he was again— that guy. Looking over his shoulder, at the camera. Looking down at the camera through the hazy glow of golden-hour light. Gazing directly into the camera and her soul. Giving the lens that Hot Guy Look.*

Now she had something to Google.

It didn't take long to find a YouTube video of the new TV commercial for Levi's jeans and many comments about the name of the hot guy who was featured in it.

Owen Brodie.

Eighteen years old.

Son of soap star Joe Brodie.

Older brother of child actor Dylan Brodie, costar of the Disney Channel hit That's So Wizard.

Younger brother of another model named Miles Brodie.

Further Googling of "Owen Brodie, model" led her to the website of his modeling agency.

She wasn't an online stalker or anything—she just liked to have information.

All the information.

She never put pictures of him up in her locker.

She never talked about him with friends.

But she did like to daydream about how they might one day meet and fall in love.

When December rolled around, she decided to send him a Christmas card, care of his modeling agency.

Why the hell not, right?

She sent him a Christmas card. It said, Hi, Owen Brodie. Just wanted to say that you're really good at what you do and I hope you're having a great life and all. Merry Christmas (if you celebrate it) and Happy New Year, and if we ever meet in the future I hope you're as nice as you look and not a total douchebag like all the other guys in Los Angeles. Love, Frances.

She was Frances back then because she wasn't cool enough to pull off being a Frankie yet.

And she felt really good about sending him that sweet, funny card.

Even when he didn't write her back.

Because she didn't even know if he got the card.

It could have been lost in the mail. The agency might not have forwarded it to him. He might have gotten it and written her back, and his card got lost in the mail.

She'd never know.

It was so romantic.

Or...it finally occurred to her that maybe he did get the card but didn't have a sense of humor. Maybe he was offended. Maybe he really was a douchebag.

She eventually decided that he was definitely a douchebag.

She took down the pictures from her wall.

She didn't tear them up or get rid of them—just in case it was taking the modeling agency a really long time to forward her card to him.

But eventually she forgot about how much she had liked him and about how much she hated him for being a douchebag, and then Justin P. asked her if she wanted to go out with him, so she barely ever thought about Owen Brodie at all.

Until she just happened to be flipping through a magazine while she was waiting for her mom at her hair salon—five years later. She saw a picture of a celebrity charity event that was attended by model and fledgling stand-up comic Owen Brodie and his very pregnant wife, Ashley.

By now, she too was a fledgling stand-up comic, so she found this hilarious.

She definitely didn't Google him once she got home.

She totally did not read every single one of his tweets on Twitter.

She absolutely did not think he was funny.

She may have gotten really, really drunk and heckled him when he dared to show up at a comedy club in Tampa.

But she certainly never expected to see him again, even once she moved to Los Angeles.

To be clear—she moved to Los Angeles for her. Not for him.

And she definitely didn't think about the way he kept looking at her in his kitchen while utilizing a percussion massage therapy device to pound away the unbearable hot, wet tension in her throbbing clitoris multiple times.

Because she can't bang her boss, especially when he's not funny, especially when he's Owen fucking Brodie.

I'll have to make up the erotic part that comes later if I ever do write this short story.

Because the erotic part isn't actually going to happen later in real life.

For many, many reasons.

OWEN

ME: *Is this funny?*
DYLAN: *No.*
ME: *I haven't gotten to the funny thing yet.*
DYLAN: *I've been waiting for you to get to the funny thing my whole life.*
MILES: *What's funny is the fact that people pay to hear you tell them what you think about things and we've always had to listen to it for free. I would pay you to stop asking me if things are funny.*
DYLAN: *<man throwing money GIF>*
ME: *Assholes.*
MILES: *When were you planning on telling me you hired a nanny?*
ME: *Who told you?*
MILES: *I ran into Martin at Soho House. You hired his 26 yr old niece to travel with you? I really hope she isn't hot.*

DYLAN: *Is she hot?*

DYLAN: *Uh oh.*

DYLAN: *She sounds hot, Miles.*

MILES: *Here's some free legal, career, and life advice from your slightly older and much wiser brother--do not have sex with her.*

DYLAN: *Definitely have sex with her.*

MILES: *Yeah, definitely take advice from the brother who bangs all of his costars.*

DYLAN: *Not all of them. Apparently I'm not Maggie Smith's type, which was very disappointing.*

MILES: *Oh hey, are you about to go on stage, Owen? Are you in Florida now?*

DYLAN: *Awww you're nervous, aren't you? What's the joke?*

MILES: *Tell us the joke, buddy.*

ME: *Fuck off, both of you.*

DYLAN: *Break a leg, bro. See you soon, right?*

MILES: *You'll kill. You've always been the second-funniest model I know. After me.*

DYLAN: *I'm definitely funnier than both of you, but break a leg.*

Fuckers.

I'm not saying I get nervous before every show, because I'm a fucking badass.

But I do start to question my act, my decision to become a professional comedian, my ability to make anyone laugh or care about what I have to say about anything, and my very existence as a human—in a really confident, masculine way.

This is my first theater tour as a headliner, so it probably wasn't a great idea to ask the Tampa Heckler to be in the audience, along with my son and over a thousand strangers. If Frankie and Sam thought I was funny, it might be a different story. If my son hadn't barfed on me right after takeoff on the four-and-a-half hour flight from LA to Tampa this morning, I might be feeling a little more baller. If I didn't have to see my former in-laws when I drop my kid off with them after the show, I might be in a better mood. If I didn't know the Tampa Heckler's parents were going to be in the audience, I might not be second-guessing every single one of my jokes.

But I have to get my head in the game. I'm playing my usual pre-show playlist on my phone. All the songs are from various *Rocky* soundtracks. Frankie's going to be bringing Sam from the hotel back here to my dressing room soon, and I don't even care that she's going to give me shit about what I'm listening to.

I may not be a seasoned comedian yet, but I've learned enough as a model that you don't put your shirt on until right before you have to perform. So I'm pacing around the room shirtless, listening to "Eye of the Tiger," running through my act in my head. Trying to get Frankie out of it.

We flew business class, so I made Sam sit next to me when we boarded the plane. But after takeoff— after he hurled—he insisted on sitting next to Frankie. Which was fine with me because the guy sitting next to her was chatting her up. So I let her trade seats with me.

Side note—the seat did not smell like vomit. I could tell Sam was nauseated, so I pulled the barf bag from the seat pocket in front of me. While I was holding the bag open for him, he leaned over in my direction and vomited *at* the paper bag. Bless his little heart, but it got on my arm and my shirt. Missed the inside of the bag and any upholstery entirely. I was so proud of him.

When Frankie and I squeezed past each other in the aisle, she made eye contact with me as her tits brushed up against my chest. This was after I had retreated to the lavatory to change out of the vomit-y shirt and spritz on some travel-size cologne. I stopped where I was. There was mild turbulence. I put my hands on her arms to steady her. We maintained eye contact.

It was a moment.

I was about three feet away from my son and thinking about joining the Mile High Club with his new nanny.

And then the moment ended abruptly. I watched as she shook her head, as if physically trying to rid herself of whatever thoughts she was having about me. She frowned, looked down at my hands, which were still holding her arms. I let go. And she hasn't made eye contact with me since then. Not at the Tampa airport. Not when I drove the rental car to the hotel. Not when we all had a bite to eat together in the hotel restaurant before I left to come to the theater.

Which is fine, I keep telling myself, because she's my manager's niece. She's going to have to make eye contact with me again at some point, since I'm her employer, but no other part of her should be making contact with me. That's a fact.

And almost as if he could read my thoughts from twenty-five hundred miles away, I get a text notification from Frankie's uncle.

MARTIN HANCOCK: *You right, mate? Checking in to see if you have everything you need for Tampa. I'm here on my mobile if you need anything. Break a leg.*
ME: *All good, thanks.*
MARTIN HANCOCK: *Good on ya. It'll be a rip snorter of a show, I know it.*
ME: *<thumbs-up emoji>*

Half the time I have no fucking clue what my manager is saying, but he gets ten percent of my income to be supportive, so I'm guessing *rip snorter* is a good thing. Also guessing I shouldn't tell him about the rip snorter of a moment between his niece and me on the plane. Or the rip snorter of a fantasy I had about her in the hotel shower before I came here today. Or the one I'll probably have when I get back to the hotel tonight, since Sam will be staying with the former in-laws and I'll have the room to myself.

Frankie has a room across the hall. She said her parents turned her old room into a gym slash craft room. So I guess I'll be driving us back to the hotel after I drop off Sam later.

And I need to get that out of my head.

My phone vibrates again, interrupting a James Brown song for a millisecond. It's a text from my mother. My parents have been back in Texas for a few years now, and they talk and text like they never left. I was born in Houston, but when I talk and text with them now, I get a bit twangy too, even though we moved to LA when I was still in daycare.

MAMA BRODIE: *Ohhh sugar, I do apologize! I've just been runnin around like a chicken with my head cut off all day long and I almost forgot to wish you a happy show tonight. <partying face emoji> You in Florida right now, sweets?*
ME: *Yes ma'am. Tampa. Here with Sam. He's coming to see the show.*
MAMA BRODIE: *Awww you give my little doodlebug three big kisses for me. I miss him so much. Now what's this I hear about a new nanny for your tour? You know your boy could of stayed here with us. Y'all better plan on*

comin to the house for supper now you hear? We're comin to see your show in Houston, you know.

POPS BRODIE: *Let the man answer, woman.*

ME: *Yes ma'am. We'll be there and I got you comps for Houston. Hey, Pops.*

POPS BRODIE: *Hey, son. Now tell your mama about this nanny so I don't have to hear her go on and on and on about it anymore.*

MAMA BRODIE: *Oh hush you. But tell me, Owen. Tell me tell me. What's her name? How old is this girl? Is she a professional caretaker? Does Sam like her? Is she pretty?*

ME: *Her name is Frankie, she is 26 and she is certified by the Red Cross for first aid and CPR. So Sam is basically safer with her than he is with me and he likes her a lot. But she's actually also a comedian. And my manager's niece.*

MAMA BRODIE: *Oh my goodness! Well now how do you like that? Another comedian. You must have so much fun together.*

POPS BRODIE: *Sounds to me like she's real pretty. What say you, Mama?*

MAMA BRODIE: *She sounds awful pretty like Miles said and I just cannot wait to meet her. Is she from LA? Do you think she'll eat chicken fried steak? I am just pleased as all git-out you finally found a nice girl for both of you boys.*

ME: *Okay I actually have to start getting dressed for the show now.*

MAMA BRODIE: *I love you to bits, you hear?*

POPS BRODIE: *Break a leg, son. Say hey to Sam for me.*
ME: *Love y'all bye.*

Two seconds after I put my phone back down, I get a text from my dad that's not a part of the group chat with my mother.

POPS BRODIE: *I agree with Miles. Do not have sex with the nanny.*
POPS BRODIE: *Break a leg.*
ME: *<thumbs-up emoji>*

Fuck me, I should have hired the old German lady with the swollen ankles who smelled like menthol. Sam was scared of her, but at least everyone, including me, would agree that I shouldn't have sex with her and I wouldn't have to do any eggplant emoji math in my head.

There's a knock at my dressing room door, and it's so sarcastic and judgmental, I don't have to ask who it is.

I open the door and find Frankie there, all glossy-lipped, wearing a pretty blouse and dark skinny jeans with sandals...holding hands with my son. My heart squeezes in my chest. She held his hand when we walked through the airport too. I don't know why it gets to me, but it does.

She's still not making eye contact with me though.

"Hey, buddy. You have a good nap?"

"Yeah. Hey."

"Come on in." I gesture for them to enter. "Welcome, Frankie," I say, daring her to look at me. "Thanks for coming."

"Uh-huh. Dressing room, huh?" She lets Sam's hand slide from hers as she looks around, at everything but my face. Or my bare chest. Because I'm still shirtless. "Nice. The room. Good size. Clean." She's blushing. And glancing at my reflection in the mirror behind me.

I'm winning this moment.

"Yeah, it's better than waiting at the bar at some comedy club. Have a seat."

Sam is, of course, already making himself comfortable on the sofa. Frankie stands exactly where she is. I casually walk past her, pick up my shirt from the back of a chair, and take my sweet-ass time putting it on and buttoning it up.

"Is that cheese?" Sam asks, staring at the small charcuterie platter on the dressing table. "Can I have it?"

He doesn't ask if he can have *some* cheese. He wants all of it.

"You can try some, see if you like it."

He scoffs, as if he's ever met a cheese he didn't

like, and waits for me to carry the platter over to him on the sofa.

"I'll get it," Frankie says, bringing him napkins and the cheese and cold cuts. "How do you get a mouse to smile?" she asks him, sitting on the sofa now and giving him all of the eye contact she refuses to give me.

"Say *cheese*," he says, smiling.

"Smart."

"Hey, what does the cheese say to himself when he's looking in the mirror?" I ask Sam as he's stuffing two pieces of sliced cheddar into his mouth—one on each side.

He shrugs.

"'Lookin' Gouda.'"

Both he and Frankie just shake their heads, not looking at me.

"What's a pirate's favorite cheese?" she asks—to Sam only.

He shrugs, but he's smiling at her when he does it.

"Chedd-*arrrrrrggghhh*."

Sam laughs with his mouth full of cheddar. It's a disgusting, happy sight.

"What do you call cheese that isn't your cheese?" I ask, totally not out of desperation.

"Nacho cheese!" Sam replies.

"Hey, yeah!"

"You've told me that one a hundred bajigglion times."

"You never remembered the answer before." I want to turn this into a father-son moment, but Frankie interrupts.

"Hey, I've got a funny pizza joke," she tells Sam.

"What?"

"Aw, never mind." She waves dismissively. "It's too cheesy."

Sam laughs at that. *Laughs.* Hard. Like it's hilarious. Like he didn't find that joke totally unfunny when I told it to him over the phone the last time we were in Tampa.

This is not what I need right before the first show of my tour—bombing in my own dressing room in front of my little asshole travel companions.

The Rocky theme, "Gonna Fly Now," starts playing on my phone.

Shit.

"Uhhh… Are you listening to the *Rocky* soundtrack to get psyched up for your show?" She grins and finally looks at me, a mischievous glint in her eyes.

"You got a problem with that?" I snap.

She's taken aback by my tone. "Not really, dude. I listen to it too, sometimes."

"You do? Before a show?"

"In the car on the way to a show. Obviously I've never had a dressing room-type situation."

I nod. "You will."

The impish grin becomes a half smile. Everything about her relaxes all of a sudden. Her brown eyes soften, sparkle with gratitude. I don't even know what to do with that look from her. She's so pretty.

We just stare at each other from across the room for what feels like an eternity, and then the phone in her back pocket vibrates. She tears her gaze away from mine, pulls the phone out, and stares down at it.

I really need to go over my set list. I walk over to the dresser to fuss with my hair and read through the bullet points.

"Shhhhark farts!"

I look back at her. She appears to be shocked about something, and it's definitely not how amazing my hair looks right now. "What?"

"Um. Why did I just get a text from my mother informing me that she and my dad just picked up their comps for your show?"

Strange question.

"So you know they're here, I'd imagine."

"But *why* are they here? I didn't tell them I'm in town, and I definitely didn't tell them I was here with you."

"You didn't? Why not?"

"For reasons. What the fffff…" She glances over at Sam. "Fart nugget!"

Sam laughs at that. Because Frankie Hogan is hilarious.

"Calm down. What's the big deal?"

"Nothing! There's no big deal."

"So why wouldn't you tell your parents that you're here?"

"I just…" She gets up and starts pacing around, dragging her fingers through her shiny dark hair, messing it up and sending frantic waves of sexy-lady hair fragrance my way. "Flurg! How did this?…"

"Martin must have told your mom about this show. Your mother is his sister, right?"

"Yes." She covers her face with her hands. "Mothertrucker!"

"He asked me to comp them."

"Uh-huh." She nods, vehemently, uncovering her face and fake-smiling like a lunatic even though her eyes are all watery. "That's great. That's totally fine. They won't be able to meet you after the show though, unfortunately."

"Oh really? Because Martin asked if they could come backstage after, and I said of course. They're on the list."

"Shrek!"

Okay, I do not need this right now.

"Can I talk to you outside for a minute?" I take her arm and pull her toward the door. "Sam, we'll be right outside in the hall."

Sam is too busy sucking Brie off his fingers to care what the crazy adults are up to.

The hall that leads to the stage is empty. I shut the door behind myself, stand in front of her, lean in until she's backed up against the wall, and whisper-yell at her, "What is your problem?"

"Nothing. What? I just don't want them to…"

"To what? Meet me?"

Her jaw tightens. Her nostrils are flaring. She straightens her spine, her shoulders, and stares me straight in the eyes. "Yes, Owen. I don't want them to meet you. Why should my parents have to meet you? Not everything is about you."

"No fucking kidding. Apparently everything is about *you* now. What is your problem with me, huh?"

"What are you—? Calm down."

I slap both my hands against the wall on either side of her head, but it doesn't seem to startle her. "*You* calm down, Frankie. Answer me." I lean right down into her face, and she isn't even blinking. "Why am I the worst stand-up comic in the history of comedy? Why do I have the most hideous face in the history of faces? Why am I the enemy of Frankie Hogan?"

Her voice is low and steady. "You seriously need to calm down and get into performance mode, Owen."

"I can't get into performance mode until you tell

me what's going on, Frankie." I stare at her mouth. Her lips part, the tiniest bit, and I feel something huge open up between us.

"You're a fucking asshole," she hisses.

"You're driving me fucking insane."

She grabs my face and kisses me.

Every single electrically charged atom of tension that has crackled and sparked in the air between us —from that comedy club three years ago through Twitter and every single room we've been in together—is suddenly released in a nuclear explosion of hungry lips and tongues.

My knee goes right up between her thighs, and she squeezes around it, bearing down. My hands are in her hair, and when she bites my lower lip and then sucks on it, I groan because I can't have a fucking eggplant emoji in my pants like this right before I have to go on stage. But her hands slide up into my hair now, and she's making these cute little crazy kitten noises while she kisses up my jaw and across my cheek, and then she moans into my mouth, and I grab her ass because *that fucking ass.*

"Fucking hell, Frankie."

"Fuck you fuck you fuck you." Now she's rocking back and forth against my thigh. *Jesus.* "Why is your thigh so fucking muscular? What are you? A gladiator?"

"What are *you*? A cowgirl?"

She nips at my chin with her teeth. "You

shouldn't shave before a show, you idiot." She drags the tip of her tongue up from the cleft in my chin to my upper lip and then goes in for such a deep kiss that I forget to breathe.

She is so wild and hot and sweet, I forget to say, *You shouldn't give me a raging hard-on right before I go on stage, you ruthless succubus-witch.*

I forget that she's the nanny and my manager's niece.

I forget that the creation of this beautiful, crazy universe between us will inevitably end with her hating me and my son hating me and me hating myself, because the warmth of her and the taste of her and the dazzling, bewildering intensity of this kiss is the best thing I've experienced in years and years and years.

Frankie fucking Hogan.

The Tampa Heckler really does want my pecker.

She pulls away from me so fast, pushes me away like she's waking up from a fever dream.

Or maybe she read my mind just now.

"Shit," she whispers.

"Fuck."

"Shit!"

"Fuuuuck."

"You have to go on in like twenty minutes."

"Oh, *do* I?" I try to pace around, but it feels like there are three legs in my pants right now. "Fuck."

"Oh no."

"How's my hair look?"

She glances up at my hair and bursts out laughing for a few glorious seconds and then covers her mouth and shakes her head. Shaking the good thoughts away again. "I'm sorry, I'm sorry. I shouldn't have done that."

"Yeah. That was the worst."

She looks down at the furious bulge in the front of my jeans, covers her mouth again. "Oh shit."

"Yeah. Just—you know what, just get Sam and go to your seats."

"Yep. On it."

I give her a look.

"I mean, *not* on it anymore. Not going anywhere near…"—she gestures toward the bulge—"it."

"Seriously, just—"

"Yup. Going. Break a leg!"

She opens the door to the dressing room, leaving me to limp around the hallway.

A stage manager appears at the other end of the hall, his eyes widening when he sees the disheveled mess of a boner I am right now.

"I'll be ready," I tell him through gritted teeth.

At least I'm not nervous anymore.

I look down at the front of my jeans. "Joke's on you, asshole."

FRANKIE

Shit.

Shit shit shit.

Fuck.

I look over at Sam, who keeps rearranging himself in his seat, trying to get comfortable. We're in the orchestra box, house left. The opening act comic is about to take the stage, and, hopefully, fifteen minutes from now, Sam's father will not pick up the mic and stand in the spotlight looking like he's got a spare mic hiding in his jeans.

"You excited to see your dad work?"

"I guess. Yeah. Can I take off my shoes?"

There's no one else in this box with us. "Sure. I don't see why not."

He starts to lean forward so he can pull off his shoes but then says to himself, "Oh yeah." He sits up straight, pulls two pieces of cheese and crackers from the front pocket of his pants, and then places them very carefully on the arm of the chair. "You can have some," he tells me, wiping his fingers on his pants and then pulling off his Vans and letting them drop to the floor.

"Thanks, buddy." I am so fond of this little dude, but I'm not touching his pocket snacks.

I pull a couple of wet wipes from my purse. When he's sitting cross-legged, he nods, confirming that he has finally achieved the perfect sitting position for a live comedy show featuring his father. I hand him one of the wipes as he's reaching for the cheese.

"Thank you. Do my feet smell?"

I sniff the air. "They smell really Gouda."

He doesn't laugh, and I realize it's because he doesn't know the names of all the cheeses. I'm just so glad his dad wasn't around to see him not laugh at me.

"What if I need to go to the bathroom when my dad is talking on the stage?"

"Just let me know, and I'll take you to the ladies' room."

He wrinkles his nose. "Will there be ladies in there?"

"Well, I ain't no lady. But I'll be in there with you."

He blinks at me, considering this. "Okay."

I finally realize my phone has been vibrating in

my pocket and I need to put it in my purse. And then I see that it's a notification from my mum and dad and remember that they're here. They're fucking here in the theater, and they're going to want to talk to Owen after the show. I had forgotten for a few minutes because I was so busy internally screaming about making out with my nemesis that I forgot to continue internally screaming about a potentially worse situation.

I mean, the kissing part was great. Stellar, really. It's the person I was kissing who was terrible. I mean, it's not like he's a terrible person, but it's terrible that I kissed him and it's worse that it was such a hot kiss.

I take that back—he is a terrible, awful person for being such a good kisser.

Shit, I need to respond to my parents' texts.

MUM: *Frances. We can see you there in the box. Stop ignoring us.*

DAD: *Hey there, peanut. Just know that we are not angry with you for lying to us regarding your whereabouts and forgoing an opportunity to visit with your loving parents who only want the best for you. We have no intention of informing this handsome comedian that he once adorned the walls of your bedroom. Unless you don't text us back immediately. Then we'll have to.*

MUM: *Don't listen to your dad, Frankie Jean. We'll be telling him no matter what. Oh and I have some very*

funny new joke ideas for you, darling! <winking face emoji>
ME: *Why do you hate me?*
DAD: *Ahhh, there she is. Welcome back to Tampa, hon.*
MUM: *You look like you just rolled out of bed...*

I comb my fingers through my hair as I scan the audience. I can't believe Owen Brodie sold out this theater three years after playing that comedy club here and I'm still doing open mics and—*oh yeah, I'm his son's nanny.* I spot my mum and dad in the fourth row, center. I spot them because they're both standing and waving at me, grinning like two devils who are going to humiliate their only daughter in about an hour and a half. I put my hands together in prayer and plead with my face. *Please don't ruin my life. Haven't I already ruined it enough myself?*

Donna Hogan blows me a kiss, and my dad winks at me.

They sit back down and ignore me.

This is not good.

ME: *I will do anything you ask, just please don't tell Owen anything.*

No response.

I look down at my parents. My dad pats at his jacket pocket, indicating that his phone is in there and he won't be texting me back. My mother pulls something out of her purse, and I watch in horror as she unfolds it. She then holds it up so I can see it. It's one of the magazine pictures of Owen that I had on my bedroom wall when I was fourteen. She probably found it in my closet when she was turning my old room into an exercise/craft room. I mentally and emotionally ripped all of them up, but I didn't have the heart to literally throw any of them away or destroy them. She makes the international gesture for "signature" at me.

I'm pretty sure they're just messing with me.

I give her the double thumbs-up.

They wouldn't do that to me.

"Hey, is that lady holding up a picture of my dad?"

"No, I don't think so. I don't know who that is. Oh, look! The opening act's coming on. Look at the stage!" I put my hands on the sides of Sam's face to turn his head away from the picture of his dad that my mum is holding.

They're definitely just messing with me.

Fifteen minutes later, and I'm still positive that this is true. My parents wouldn't humiliate me with Owen just because I didn't tell them I'm in town overnight this one time. I'm the asshole in this family, not them.

Owen Brodie saunters onstage, without any evidence of boner. I mean, he probably bangs women to the *Rocky* theme before every show, for all

I know. His hair is just a bit mussed up, and he's wearing his glasses. He looks so cute I want to throw things at him. And run my fingers through his hair again before slapping him.

He takes the microphone off the stand, waits for the applause to die down just a little, and then launches into it.

"Thanks for coming, everyone. So good to be back in Tampa. A lot's happened since I was last here. You've gained a legendary quarterback and won a Super Bowl..." He waits for the easy applause and cheers to die down before continuing. "I've learned that gator jokes are not funny and gotten divorced. So we're both doing great. My seven-year-old son is actually here tonight. He doesn't think I'm funny, and he's absolutely right. I won't point him out to you because he doesn't like being pointed at or stared at, and he also doesn't like it when I tell him jokes, which is too bad because I'm going to tell a bunch of jokes that I already know he hates. Starting now. This is the first post-divorce joke I told him... Hey, Sam—that's his name—what's black and white and pink all over?... Your Animaniacs T-shirt that I just washed with your new Spider-Man pajamas."

People laugh because he's being all humble and relaxed and cute.

Even Sam is laughing. I record this for Owen on

my phone. The sound of his son laughing along with around a thousand strangers.

He's not doing the stupid "Hi, I'm handsome" jokes anymore. He's just handsome.

I don't know why that makes me even angrier, but I stop recording and text the voice memo to Owen's phone. Not as a comedian who's funnier than he is but as a nanny who doesn't care if he's funny or handsome or not—she just needs a paycheck.

"I've got a document on my laptop called *Fart Jokes for Sam* because you would think that comedian fart jokes smell the funniest, but it turns out mine just stink. Don't they, Sam?"

He's doing an entire bit on jokes that bombed with his son, and it's cute and he's killing.

I'm happy for him. I am. The tightness in my chest means I'm happy for him. Just like the tightness in my clitoris means I'm glad I'm wearing jeans instead of a skirt tonight.

"You okay in there, buddy?"

I don't want to be that person who rushes a child to finish using the toilet just because he's picked the actual worst time in the history of my life to have to go to the bathroom, but he's been in that stall for five minutes and I need to get out there to head my parents off at the pass.

There's a line of about ten women waiting for three stalls. They're all smiling and talking about how funny and hot Owen Brodie is. I can't listen to it. Not because I don't want to hear it but because I'm realizing that Owen Brodie's son is groaning because he has the cheese poops.

"There isn't enough toilet paper in here," he grunts.

"Okay, hang on." I pull a handful of Kleenex from my purse. As a certified babysitter, I am literally prepared for this shit. I hold my breath, crouch down in front of Sam's stall, reach my hand out to him under the door, and wait for him to take the Kleenex from me.

"I can't reach."

I bend down a little lower so I can hold it up a little higher.

"I still can't."

I crouch down on my knees and smush my face up against the stall door until I feel the Kleenex leave my hands, and then I jump up, step back, and inhale again.

"You okay now? We gotta go, buddy."

"I don't think I should leave the toilet."

"There's a toilet where your dad is. We'll just run over there, and you can hop back on." I don't want to say *backstage* because then people will figure out this is Owen's son and want to talk to him and it will take even longer to get back there.

I hear the toilet flush, praise the digestive lords, whip out a couple of antibacterial wet wipes, and get ready to sprint.

Sam comes out of the stall. I wipe his hands for him, take one of them in mine, and haul him out of the ladies' room, through the lobby, to the entrance of the backstage area. It takes somewhere between nine seconds and forever.

And I'm too fucking late.

When we get to Sam's dressing room, the door is open and my parents are in there. They're both laughing. Not evil *bwahahahaha we just ruined our only daughter's life* kind of laughs, but delighted, adoring laughter. Like they're laughing about how funny his show was, maybe.

Maybe I'm still the only asshole in this family, I'm thinking, as I let go of Sam's hand and catch my breath and see that...Owen is at his dresser, writing on the old magazine ad of him with a Sharpie. While smirking.

"Hey, Frances," he says, not even looking over at me. He signs his name with an obnoxious flourish, turns to face me, and carefully holds the torn-out page to me. Like a peace offering. But with a smirk. Which means he thinks he has something on me. He doesn't. What he doesn't know is that I don't like him anymore. So none of this means anything.

I don't look at what he wrote. I just fold up the piece of paper and slip it into my back pocket. I totally ignore the flicker of disappointment across his smirky face when he realizes I'm not going to read what he wrote.

But he gets over it quickly enough when he realizes Sam is in the room. The way he watches his son, hesitantly trying to read whether or not he enjoyed the performance, isn't adorable at all.

I go over to my parents to hug them, even though they are terrible, horrible people.

"Hey, buddy," Owen says to Sam. "You stay awake for the whole show?"

"Yeah. It was fun."

"Yeah? You had a good time?"

"Yeah. I had cheese poops after, but I laughed at some of the jokes. It was good."

"I'm so glad, Sam. Thanks for coming." He holds up his fist for Sam to fist bump him.

I am in no way moved by this tiny father-son moment.

"You need to use the bathroom in here?"

"Nah, I'm okay."

"So this is the famous son, Sam," my dad says. "I got a question for you. What does a ninja fart sound like?"

Sam shrugs.

"Nothin'."

Sam just stares at him for a couple of seconds.

"Ninja *fahts* are silent but deadly," my mum adds by way of explanation, but also the way she says *fahts* is hilarious.

Sam laughs. Hard. He loves ninjas. I've only known him for a short while, but I already know all of the things he likes: ninjas, cheese, naps, documentaries about wild animals killing each other, Spider-Man, and me. And maybe his dad, a little bit.

I'm thinking about how much more he likes me than his dad, how little I like his dad. I'm thinking about how I don't even care what his dad wrote on that print ad and how I will definitely never kiss that smug asshole again, when I catch the look on Sam's face and know from the very still way he's standing that he just laughed so hard he sharted.

And suddenly, nothing matters more than the fact that it is my job to calmly lead Sam to the bathroom without causing him any embarrassment and then ask his father to get a change of undies from the suitcase that's in the rental car.

I bet we'll all be ready to joke about it by tomorrow.

What's yellow and black and white and blue and brown all over?

Sam's Minion underpants after he sharted.

14

OWEN

I need to work all this into my act. I mean, if this night doesn't just define my life as a single dad comic, then I don't know what does. Get yacked on by son on the flight here. Make out with nanny right before show. Tell fart jokes to around a thousand grown-ups during show. Find out the greatest black-mail material about hot snarky nanny direct from her parents backstage, followed by ninja fart joke-induced sharting by son and aftermath. I don't know what the punchline is yet, but I'm pretty sure it won't involve more making out with the hot, snarky nanny.

What I mean is—it *won't* involve more making out with the hot snarky nanny.

I should not be thinking about sex with the nanny after dealing with Sam's underpants circumstance together, but the way she handled the whole situation was just so gracious. She was patient and understanding and good humored and hot, and I'm so grateful I want to thank her by fucking her with my tongue and my fingers and my cock and my words and literally any other way she wants me to fuck her—I would do it.

There are other ways to show my gratitude, and I will have to remember what they are when I'm not so fucking aroused, but I would rather do it the tongue/finger/cock/filthy-talk way.

I'm thinking this two seconds after walking out of my former in-laws' house and saying good night to my son. He is not happy that he has to spend the night with them, and I don't blame him. But he'll be sleeping most of the time—after taking a butt bath—so he'll be fine. Frankie stayed in the car. Once again, she's not making eye contact with me.

She probably still hasn't read what I wrote on that old magazine ad because she's such a stubborn asshole.

But at least I have some context now for the stubborn assholery.

It's not easy, but I'll try not to be too cocky about it.

I won't try very hard, but I'll try.

She's sitting in the passenger seat of my rental car, staring straight ahead. I get in and start the engine, saying nothing. The radio comes on automatically, but I turn it off. Just to make her even more uncomfortable.

After another minute of huff-filled silence, as I follow the GPS app's directions to the hotel, I finally say with great enthusiasm, "Your parents are great."

She covers her face and mumbles, "Shut up."

"I'm not even talking about how they told me you were obsessed with me when you were fourteen."

"Stop."

"I'm talking about how nice and funny they are. I'm not even jealous that Sam thinks your whole family is funnier than I am. But thanks for sending me that voice memo, by the way. That was good to hear."

"Sure." She slaps the palms of her hands on her thighs, shaking her head. "Sorry my dad made your son poop his pants."

"I'm sure the janitor has found worse things in that dressing room than poop-stained underpants."

"Like your set-list." She barks out a laugh. "Sorry. I had to say it. But it was a great show."

"Asshole."

"No, really. It was fun." She seems to genuinely believe this, which is nice.

"I know."

"Well, you can't be all that big of a deal since you don't even have a limo."

"I actually told Martin to cancel the limo drivers when I have Sam with me. He doesn't like it when there's a stranger driving. But I'm glad you think I'm awesome now."

"I mean, it was better than the last time I saw your act, but get over yourself."

"I am over myself. You're the one who needs to get over me."

She shakes her head again. No response. She just looks out the passenger window.

"Have you read what I wrote—"

"No."

"Read it."

"No."

"I can just tell you what I wrote."

"No—so I see you've taken your glasses off. Do you just wear them for your act now? To make yourself seem like a more likable person?"

"Yes. You should get a pair."

She finally glances over at me for a second. "Do you even need glasses?"

"Yes. But I know better than to wear them when you're always one comment away from punching me in the face."

"Surely I'm not the only one. But it's good that you wear them for your act. I still think you should abstain from shaving."

"I'll be abstaining from plenty of things on this trip, don't worry about it."

"So will I. You also don't have to worry about it."

"I'm not worried. I'm relieved. The last thing I need is my nanny trying to ride the D train before I have to go onstage."

"Hey, my hands didn't get anywhere near the track—they weren't even in the neighborhood. Not my fault the D train left the station."

"The anaconda gets restless before a show even when I'm alone, so maybe *you* should get over yourself."

"Ahhh yes." She sighs. "We're familiar with anaconda problems here in Florida."

"Oh, there's no problem with my anaconda, baby. I realize you have little to no experience with real men, but our trouser snakes do exactly what we need them to do—*when* we need them to do it."

"I happen to have plenty of experience with pants pythons, and there's a reason I stay away from men who refer to themselves as 'real men.'"

"Seriously—why do you have so much resistance toward me?"

"What?"

"You heard me."

"I know, but who asks that kind of thing?"

"Grown-ups. Ever dated one?"

She frowns at me. "I date adult men, yes."

"Not exactly what I meant, and you know it."

"I mean…"

"Right. Let me guess. Your last boyfriend had two

roommates, wore leather bracelets, and made minimum wage, but he was great at going down on you."

"Wrong. He was a staff writer on a TV show, had his own apartment, and his mouth skills were subpar. But the guy I dated before the last guy was a bartender and a very good kisser."

"Did they even take you out on dates, or did you just Netflix and chill?"

"What is your point?"

Good question. What is your point, Owen? Because it was supposed to be that you're not going to have sex with her.

"Only that you deserve better and you might be afraid of falling for someone who could actually take care of you... I'm not talking about *me*. I'm just saying. You're not as terrible a person as you seem to want people to believe you are. So maybe you should be on the lookout for someone with a well-developed life *and* love muscle."

She is silent for about ten seconds, staring straight ahead.

It does nothing to stop my magic wand from wanting to cast a spell on her chamber of secrets because I can hear how hard she's breathing. But we both need to *arresto momentum*.

"Let's not talk for the rest of the way," she says.

"Great idea. Let's not talk for the rest of the night."

"Fantastic idea."

I turn on the radio.

The Stones song "(I Can't Get No) Satisfaction" is playing.

And there's the punchline.

15

FRANKIE

The only thing that has ever felt longer than that fifteen-minute drive from dropping Sam off with his grandparents to dropping the rental car off with valet parking at this hotel is this elevator ride up to our rooms.

It's taking fifteen years to get from the lobby to the tenth floor and I'm as far away from Owen as I can be in here, but somehow even after getting barfed on and touching poopie underpants, that man still smells amazing, and I need to get the fuck out of here before I hump his leg again.

"You happy with your room?" he asks.

"Yes. Very. Thank you."

"You're welcome. Does it have a view of the bay?"

"No. I'm not inviting you in to see it."

"I'm not interested in seeing it. As you saw when you were with Sam, my suite does have a very nice

146

view of the bay. You gonna hang out in your room tonight?"

"I'm pretty tired, so I think I'll just take a bath and go to bed."

"Sounds good. I'm still pretty wired, so I'll probably head down to that hotel bar."

"Interesting."

"Is it?" He shrugs.

"The one on the patio?"

"Yup."

"The one with the big group of drunk ladies in tube tops?"

"They weren't all that drunk." He arches a very well-groomed eyebrow. "Care to join me?"

"No, sir."

"Are you sure? Because it seems like you don't want me going down there by myself."

"I couldn't care less what you get up to tonight."

The elevator finally dings at the tenth floor, and the doors open. I step out and walk down the hall so fast, trying to get the image of Owen having a twelve-way with those obnoxious, tube top-wearing, hammered—

"Wrong way, Captain."

I stop in my tracks and turn around without looking at him. I don't need to see that smug face again tonight. We said we weren't going to talk for the rest of the night.

This is bullshit.

"Y'know," he says as he reaches the door to his suite. I'm still not looking at his smug face, but I can tell he's smirking because he sounds so damn smug and smirky. "I think maybe I'll just hang out in my room too."

"Like I said, I couldn't care less what you do."

"I can tell."

"Good night," I say in the way that a super chill person who totally doesn't care what another person does with his penis would say it. "Thank you for comping my parents." I try to open the door to my room with the keycard, but it gives me the red light.

"That was really my pleasure."

I try the stupid keycard again, and it gives me the stupid red light again.

"Would you like some help with that?"

"No thank you."

"I just feel like—as the man who used to be the guy whose face plastered your bedroom wall when you were a teenager—I should be the man who teaches you how to use a keycard properly."

I am paralyzed with humiliation and rage when I feel his chest press up against my back. He takes my hand, which is still holding the stupid fucking keycard, lifts it up right above the swipe reader, and gently swipes it through. His hand is big and warm and probably moisturized with male model lotion, and I want him to put that thing on all of my lady things—*fuck you, Owen Brodie.* The green light goes on in my ovaries and on the swipe reader, and there's probably a quiet clicking sound from the door, but I can't hear it because of all the loud swear words in my head.

"Thank you so much. Have a good night."

"That was also my pleasure, and good night to you too."

He's still standing in the same spot when I go inside and let the door close.

"Don't forget to read what I wrote to you."

"Uh-huh!"

I pull the folded-up magazine page from my back pocket and slap it down on top of the dresser without unfolding it.

There's a fancy bottle of red wine on the dresser, a wineglass, a bottle opener, and a small envelope with my name on it. Beside them, a note from the front desk tells me that this was ordered for me while I was out. I open the envelope. The front of the card has the logo from the hotel bar on it. Inside the card, it says:

Called the hotel to have this delivered to your room because I thought you and your inner fourteen-year-old might need it. Cheers! ;) OWEN

Did he tell them to add the winky face emoticon?

Would I still be humiliated, confused, and enraged if the card had not included a winky face?

149

When did he even have time to call and order this? When he left the dressing room to get a change of clothes for Sam? When he was at his in-laws' house?

Is that winky face being smug or flirtatious or both?

I don't care anymore because I'm going to get my inner fourteen-year-old drunk.

But I gotta hand it to him—this was a classy dick move.

I pour myself a full glass and finish half of it before pulling my phone out and taking a seat at the chair next to the side table.

I am definitely not about to check Twitter to see if Owen tweeted anything since I turned off push notifications for his account. I am certainly not about to text him either, even though I should probably thank him for the wine. Fortunately, there's a text from Mia, so I don't have to do anything Owen-related on my phone at all.

MIA: *Hi! Are you in Tampa! Did you see the show?! It's so quiet in the apartment without you here. Even when you aren't talking it's like I can hear your funny negative thoughts. LOL*
ME: *Can you hear the negative thoughts I'm having about Owen Brodie right now?*
MIA: *Uh oh! What happened?!*
ME: *Pretty much the worst things that could ever happen.*

MIA: *Multiple things?! Did you have sex and realize you're in love with him?*
ME: *Absolutely not.*
MIA: *Did you fart while having sex with him and then murder him because you were so embarrassed?*
ME: *NO! I did not have sex with him.*
MIA: *So just the fart and murder then? LOL*
ME: *I wish.*
MIA: *Awww. You aren't going to tell me, are you?*
ME: *Maybe on my deathbed. In a month. When I have to find yet another job. Unless I get fired from this one before the end of the tour. But how are you?!*
MIA: *All is well and I'm heading out to a movie. Miss you!*
ME: *Miss you.*
MIA: *Let me know when you have sex with Owen Brodie and realize you're madly in love with him.*
ME: *<raised middle finger emoji>*
MIA: *LMAO*

I'm so glad *someone* can laugh her ass off about this.

I fill the tub for a bath, pour more wine for myself, and casually check my Twitter app while removing my clothes.

Owen Brodie @theowenbrodie
Thanks for the laughs, Tampa! ;) #FartJokes #ReadWhatIWrote

151

I will not be reading what he wrote.
I will not give him more reasons to gloat.
I will not read it in the bath.
I will not let him fuel my wrath.
Even now that I'm squeaky clean
That note he wrote will go unseen.
Whatever it is, I need not know.
I stopped caring about him so long ago.
…
Oh, fuck it.

I swipe the magazine page from the dresser, unfold it, and read what that asshole Owen Brodie wrote.

Dear Frances,
If I had seen any pics of you when I was fourteen, I would have put them up on my walls too.
Not pics of you when you were ten—you know what I mean.
My agency never forwarded any Christmas cards to me.
If they had sent me yours, I would have written you back.
It would have meant a lot to me.
Glad you found such a straightforward way to get your message across to me eventually anyway.
Owen Brodie

Shit.

16

OWEN

MAMA BRODIE: *How was the show, sweets?! I follow the #OwenBrodie on the tits and the Insta.*

MAMA BRODIE: **The Twitter! Whoops!*

POPS BRODIE: *Why don't you have another cocktail, Bonnie Lyn?*

DYLAN: *Welp. Now I know what I'll be talking about in therapy next week.*

MAMA BRODIE: *Oh hush, you two. What I was saying, Owen, is that I'm seeing so many positive posts about you tonight!*

MILES: *For a change.*

DYLAN: *She follows #DylanBrodie too FYI so don't let it go to your head or anything.*

MAMA BRODIE: *I follow all my boys' hashtags. And #PatrickDempsey*

POPS BRODIE: *I will kick his feeble ass next time I see him.*

ME: *It was good, Mama. Can't complain. There was a cheese poop incident right afterward, but nothing unprecedented.*

DYLAN: *Have I taught you nothing, bro? Never eat cheese before a live show. Serves you right.*

MILES: *That's one way to ensure the hot nanny won't have sex with you.*

ME: *It was Sam, not me. Assholes.*

MILES: *#IDoNotBelieveYou*

POPS BRODIE: *I'm just proud of you for staying regular, son. Maybe increase your fiber intake though.*

MAMA BRODIE: *I am mighty proud of you too, Owen. <bouquet emoji> <bottle with popping cork emoji>But definitely up the fiber intake.*

ME: *Thanks everyone. Except Dylan and Miles and maybe Pops.*

POPS BRODIE: *<face blowing a kiss emoji>*

MILES: *<cheese wedge emoji>*

DYLAN: *<pile of poop emoji>*

I hear a knock at the door to my hotel room. Been waiting for a knock at my door for an hour, but what I'm hearing is so quiet it could be from down the hall. I turn down the volume on the YouTube video I was watching on my laptop. There's another series of knocks, this time loud and impatient and kind of snarky.

It is, of course, a terrible idea to be alone in a hotel room with the nanny who is also my high-powered manager's niece. Especially after I've had a couple of beers and she has probably had some wine. But I'm not exactly going to turn her away, now that she's no doubt realized what an amazing and thoughtful guy I am. I'll just let her thank me from the hallway and then politely say good night. I'm also not going to turn off the music I've had on ever since I got back. It just happens to be the playlist Dylan made for me when I became officially divorced. It's called "Bonerific Slow Jamz." It has some great songs on it, and I happen to like listening to it after shows. Helps me to wind down.

When I finally open the door, Frankie is already turning and stepping away.

So impatient.

"Hello. What can I do for you?"

She rolls her eyes as she steps back to face me. She's not wearing any makeup, and she's so fucking pretty it hurts to look at her. "Hello." She waves a hand dismissively, then pushes a few loose strands of long, dark hair behind her ear. It's up in a ponytail again, and I want to tug on it again. Especially when her big, brown eyes dip down ever so subtly to check out my tight, white T-shirt and gray sweatpants. She just happens to be wearing exactly the same thing, and neither of us has got a bra on. She clears her throat. "I just wanted to thank you for the wine."

"You're very welcome."

"And for what you wrote on the thing."

I cross my arms in front of my chest, flexing my biceps and accentuating my pecs as I lean against the doorframe. "The magazine ad of me that you used to have up on your wall when you were fourteen? That thing?"

She huffs at me, spins on her heel, and takes three angry steps across the hall.

"Come in and hang out with me."

"No."

"Suit yourself."

She tries and fails to open the door with her keycard. Her shoulders drop in defeat. "Fine."

"No, do your thing. I'm sure you're having way more fun by yourself over there."

She turns, frowning at me, stomps over. I move to let her pass. She walks straight over to the armchair by the window and takes a seat, staring at me hard, like we're about to start negotiations.

In a way, I suppose we are.

I let the door close and go back to the sofa.

"Can I get you anything from the minibar or room service?"

"No thank you. I won't be staying long."

"Sounds good. Have a nice bath?"

"Excellent."

I take a seat and pull my laptop onto my lap. "Cool. I was just watching your acts on YouTube again."

Her eyes widen. "You were?"

"You're really funny. I like this one."

"Which one?"

"Come see." I un-pause the video so she can hear herself. It's the bit where she asks if any of the women in the audience had a real orgasm when they were in high school.

"Oh God, no. I hate watching and listening to myself. Turn it off!"

"No."

She crosses over to join me on the sofa, plopping down right next to me as she reaches for the track-pad, trying to pause the video. "I'm begging you to stop!"

"Why?" I make a half-assed attempt at blocking her, but I let her stop the video.

"I told you!" She sits back and covers her face. "Why do you do this to me?"

A D'Angelo song starts up, and I see what it does to her body, almost immediately. I have never been so grateful to my little brother for anything in my life.

"I like that bit. The songs are great. They must kill."

She lets her hands drop to her lap. "They should, shouldn't they?" She's smiling. I hardly ever get to see her like this.

"You're so fucking pretty when you smile." *Shit. That was out loud. Can't take it back now.* "I wish you did it more when you look at me."

157

I catch something that resembles a spark of appreciation flicker across her expression. Just a flicker. Something genuine. A visual whisper of encouragement to keep going. She keeps smiling, revealing a dimple, and bites her lower lip. I want those lips on mine again, I want to hear her make those sounds again, I want to see what she's been holding back again, and I've got no choice but to get out there and risk bombing.

I place the laptop next to me and turn to face her, leaning in just a bit. "You really never had an orgasm when you made out with guys in high school?"

Her eyes search mine, those lips curl up to one side, and I'm ready for any answer she'll give me. Except: "Seriously? This is your move?"

And I'm out. "No. That's not my move. Is that *your* move?" I sit back. "Do you heckle every guy who tries to make a move on you or just the men who aren't named Justin?"

Suddenly, she's straddling me and holding my face with both hands. I can't remember what she said to piss me off. My hands are on her hips, and I'm staring up into lust-filled eyes.

"You're the only man I heckle."

"What a fucking honor." I squeeze her hips and that small move elicits a sigh, and I'm in trouble.

Her lips smash against mine again. I guess there's no other way for her to start kissing me, and I'm fine with that. Her tongue tastes like Malbec and spearmint and sarcasm. The frenzy eventually gives way to breathless kisses planted all over my face. It almost feels like love, and I get that ache again, even though I know that's not what this is. Not yet.

We're just messing around, and that's fine.

Healthy, even.

Just a little funny business between two hot, funny grown-ups who need to blow off some steam when the kid's not around.

She starts rocking back and forth the tiniest bit. She's hardly even bearing down on my cock and there's barely any friction between our sweatpants, but I'm still really hard and totally fucked. "I never had actual sex in high school, okay? I just made out with guys. It's not possible for a girl to orgasm just from making out."

"Wanna bet?"

"I'm not going to have sex with you, and our clothes are staying on."

And the negotiations are in full swing.

This is gonna hurt.

"My hands need to go under your clothes."

"Acceptable. As long as you don't see anything."

"Not a problem. But you need to keep your hands away from the hammer if you don't want to get nailed tonight."

"I think I can manage to keep my hands off your junk, Head Shot."

"Famous last words. I apologize in advance for

how mad you're going to get when you find out how good I can make you feel."

"Shut up and prove it."

I tug on that ponytail and kiss her neck, licking up to a spot just below her ear. She goes limp for a second, whispers, "Holy shit," and I need to slow down or I'm going to win this bet in less than a minute.

"What do I win when I make you come, Frankie?"

I drag my fingernails down her back and squeeze her ass. She shivers and grabs hold of my shirt with both hands, eyes still closed. "You'll see," she says in a casual, sing-song way, swaying to the music.

I'll see.

She is so hot, and I am so fucking fucked.

I kiss her mouth and rub the smooth skin of her hips between the waistband of her sweatpants and the bottom of her T-shirt, barely touching her. I can feel her reaction to every touch, every move I make. So much energy. Still the slightest bit of restraint. My thumbs make their way to her belly, slowly circling. She's just a little bit soft there, and I like that a lot. She leans back, resting her hands on my knees, offering those perky tits up to me. I massage her breasts over her shirt, kissing them through the fabric.

She moans quietly, her hands messing up my hair, and I am so fucking fucked.

As far as I can tell, if this woman is awake, she's

in the excitement stage of the sexual-response cycle. So what kind of losers did she make out with in high school if they couldn't get her off?

"You sure you don't want me to take your shirt off?"

"No renegotiating," she mutters.

I bite at the fleshy part of her tit—not hard but enough to make her gasp.

If you're gonna be like that.

I give her a little spank on that ass because she needs one, and she confirms just how much she wanted it by shuddering and catching her breath and squeezing my biceps.

She squeezes her thighs together, rocking harder and faster.

My erection is right up there between them, and I am so fucking fucked.

I slip my hands up under her shirt, tease her hard nipples with my thumbs.

Her hands cover mine. My eyes are hooded and blurry with desire, but I can't stop watching her. She can barely keep her head up, and she's whimpering.

I'm doing this to her.

She's so close, and I want to feel just how wet she is for me.

I cup the back of her head with one hand, kissing her deeply as I slide the other hand into her panties.

I can feel lace and then cotton and then sweet fucking slippery warm hot heaven.

I massage her clit, and she's already jerking and trembling and crying out.

"Baby, you feel so good."

She lets out a little high-pitched yelp.

"This is killing me, Frankie. I need to be inside you."

"I know. You can't."

She presses down on my shoulders, lifts herself up, and I let two fingers slip inside her and fuck her with them if that's all she wants.

"That's what you want?"

"Yeah."

She arches back, and here she comes.

"That's all you want?"

"Owen. Oh my God."

Fucking hell.

"Say my name again."

"Owen! Fuck. Oh my God, yes."

"Yeah?"

She writhes around on my hand, grinding down on my hard cock.

"Yeah."

She cries out.

Not my name.

Not *Oh God*.

Not *fuck*.

Just this beautiful, sexy fucking sound that nearly puts me over the edge too.

This is hotter than every experience I had with all those girls in high school combined.

I grip her waist with one hand and place my fingers flat against her clit until she finally stops bucking against me.

She goes still, and I don't know where she is in her head, but I don't want her to leave me yet.

"Frankie…"

"Mmmm." Her head rolls around languidly. She rubs her lips together.

This young woman is a powerhouse of sensuality, and she hides it most of the time.

I pull my hand out just as she dips down to kiss me.

It was honestly so satisfying watching and hearing her come for me that I might be able to live without fucking her tonight.

"You win," she whispers between kisses.

"I'd say we both did." I probably should have kept that one in the old brain box, but fuck it. We both did.

And it seems we're both about to win again because she climbs off me to kneel beside me on the sofa, and now her hand is slipping down under my sweatpants and inside my boxer briefs.

Fuck me, she's giving me a slow-and-steady hand job like it's no big deal, and I am so fucking fucked.

"Does that feel good?"

"Yeah, baby. Really good."

I could cry, it feels so good.

She somehow knows exactly what I like. Cups the head with the palm of her sweet hand, twisting a little, and then strokes down the shaft and back up again. Alternately gentle and firm and gradually speeding things up. She moves with me like she's into it, and that is so hot.

She leans in and catches my earlobe between her teeth and then sucks on it just as she ramps things up, and I come so hard I might go blind and it would be worth it.

Frankie fucking Hogan.

She keeps her hand there until I'm emptied out.

I was not expecting that.

"Jesus."

I want to thank her. It would be so cheesy to thank her, but I'm so grateful right now.

She kisses my cheek before pulling her hand out.

"Be right back," she says.

"Don't go."

"I said I'll be right back."

I watch her go into the bathroom. I hear the water run. I hear her removing Kleenex from the box. I hear the water running again. And then she comes back out with a hand towel.

"I would have gotten that," I say, and then I'm rendered speechless because she sits next to me and uses the damp towel to clean me up. Wordlessly. Like it's no big deal.

It's a small gesture, I guess, but it's been so long since I've felt what it's like to have a woman take care of me like this.

Now I want to fucking cry again.

How does this woman go from being a sassy asshole to being the kindest woman I know in the span of a day?

My head is spinning.

"Owen."

"Yeah?"

She folds up the towel and stares down at it. "I know this is a really bad idea, but I really think we should just get it over with and fuck each other right now. When you're ready."

"I think you're right on both counts, and I'm ready."

She smiles. Such a pretty smile. "Good."

And then the Prince song that was playing on my phone through the Bluetooth speaker turns into the *Jaws* theme.

"Shit."

"What is happening?"

"It's my mother-in-law. Former mother-in-law." I look around for my phone.

"It's on the bed," Frankie tells me.

I know even before I answer that Sam isn't sleeping and he wants me to pick him up.

I look over at Frankie before answering, and I can tell that she knows it too.

165

I turn off the Bluetooth speaker and answer. "Hello?"

Frankie leaves the folded-up towel on the sofa, pulls her keycard out of her pocket, waves at me, and goes out the door.

I am so fucking fucked.

17

OWEN: *Does finger banging and a handy count as sex if you aren't in high school? I may have screwed up.*

MAMA BRODIE: *Well now, I suppose that depends on a few factors, hon. Degrees of nudity for either party, level of sexual satisfaction for the finger-banged party, levels of intoxication for both parties, amount of intimate kissing, etc.*

OWEN: *Oh shit. Thought this was the brothers-only group.*

DYLAN: *Now THAT was funny.*

MILES: *My expert legal advice is that you have screwed up in many, many ways, Owen. Well played.*

OWEN: *I am so sorry, Mama.*

MAMA BRODIE: *Nothing to be ashamed of, sweets. We have always raised you boys to have healthy sex lives.*

POPS BRODIE: *We just forgot to teach y'all how to*

have healthy love lives. What the shit, son? You couldn't wait until the end of the tour?

MAMA BRODIE: *Do not listen to him, sweets. Miles told me her name and I've started following your girl on the tits. She is adorable.*

MAMA BRODIE: *Oopsie! *Twitter.*

OWEN: *Not my girl. How does Miles know her name?*

MILES: *Martin told me.*

MAMA BRODIE: *I Googled her last night.*

DYLAN: *So did Owen, apparently.*

MAMA BRODIE: *Her YouTube videos are just delightful! You should have her wide open for you.*

OWEN: *Uhhh...*

MAMA BRODIE: *I meant open for you. Your stand-up show.*

POPS BRODIE: *May I pour you another mimosa, dear?*

OWEN: *Thanks as always for your input, everyone. Let's not talk about this anymore.*

POPS BRODIE: *Try to refrain from giving the nanny your input, loverboy. At least until you aren't her employer anymore.*

MILES: *Agreed, Pops. Keep it in your pants, Owen. Like the cheese poops.*

DYLAN: *So mad I didn't get to make that joke.*

OWEN: *Hey. Not sure what the protocol is for texting/calling after what we did last night. But we won't*

*be able to talk about this at breakfast with Sam around, so
I'll just say... Thanks for letting me touch ur boobs and
stuff. That was hot.*

FRANKIE: *Yeah. Ur the Dave Chappelle of making out.
But we can't do that again.*

OWEN: *Which part?*

FRANKIE: *All of it.*

OWEN: *Agree to disagree.*

FRANKIE: *I'm serious. We need to establish ground
rules.*

OWEN: *Another negotiation. All righty. Sam isn't up yet,
so we can discuss this on here now if you'd like.*

FRANKIE: *No kissing no touching no hot-guy looks no
flirting no anaconda-related banter no interactions of any
kind when either or both of us have consumed any
amount of alcohol no sexual tension-inducing behavior of
any kind in general.*

OWEN: *Literally everything we say and do creates
sexual tension.*

FRANKIE: *Owen, we can't do this. You're my uncle's
client. I can't risk messing up your relationship with him-
-he already thinks I'm a huge screw up.*

OWEN: *Martin doesn't have to know. Nobody needs to
know.*

FRANKIE: *Owen.*

OWEN: *I like hearing you say my name when I make
you feel good.*

FRANKIE: *Excellent example of things you should never
say to me.*

OWEN: *Do you deny that I made you feel good?*

FRANKIE: *No, but I resent it.*

OWEN: *Fine. We can follow your rules until we get to New York. But then I'm taking you out.*

FRANKIE: *No way.*

OWEN: *Yes way. When Sam's with my brother. I'm going to be in a music video that my friend Nico's shooting in New York. Our friend Alex is directing it. There's an after-party that night. You'll be my date.*

FRANKIE: *Agree to disagree.*

FRANKIE: *Wait. You mean Nico Todd?*

OWEN: *Yes, but he's happily married so don't even think about heckling him, missy.*

FRANKIE: *<smirking face emoji> What about Alex? That's Alex Vega, right?*

OWEN: *Also happily married.*

FRANKIE: *Well, I'm supposed to meet up with some girlfriends in NYC if I have any free time, so.*

OWEN: *You'll join me at the party after you see your friends then.*

FRANKIE: *This is not the kind of negotiation I had intended.*

OWEN: *This part is non-negotiable. It's an order.*

OWEN: *Shit. Sam's up. He wants cheese.*

FRANKIE: *Not before a flight!*

OWEN: *Roger that. See you at the restaurant in twenty?*

FRANKIE: *Roger that.*

OWEN: *;)*

FRANKIE: *Stop it.*

OWEN: *<winking face emoji>*

OWEN: *Shit. He had pocket cheese. Ate it when I wasn't looking. We gotta make sure he eats a lot of dry toast for breakfast or something.*

FRANKIE: *That'll teach you to wink at me.*

OWEN: *;)*

18

FRANKIE HOGAN JOKE
NOTEBOOK - JULY, ENTRY 2

Shit.

I got nothin'.

What if I can't think of anything funny when Owen Brodie is being nice to me and my clitoris?

What if he kissed all the angst-based humor away and now I'm just going to be some well-adjusted, happy person for the rest of my life? What the fuck am I supposed to do for an act? Observational humor? Hey, have you ever noticed how garbanzo beans look like tiny butts? What's up with that?

What's up with how much I liked it when Owen spanked my butt? Why hasn't anyone else done that to me before? What if he spanked the sass out of me?

What if I'm only funny when I date idiots named Justin?

What if my entire act and personality was fueled by

my silent rage against Owen Brodie ignoring me when I was a teenager?

Why do I still have tiny micro-orgasms every time I think about him?

When will I stop feeling the ghost of his monster erection between my legs?

When will my vulva stop screaming at me for not getting up on that thing again?

How would it feel to actually have that thing inside me? Better, right? So good.

Where did he learn to kiss like that? It literally is not funny, how good a kisser he is.

Why should anyone be allowed to look that good and smell that good and kiss that well and be a good dad and have a successful career and make me feel that good and ruin my fucking life by being so sweet to me and my boobs?

Who does he think he is?

Maybe he's terrible at going down on women. I should find out. If he's bad at it, I would find a lot of humor in that. I would love that. I would never stop laughing.

Wait—am I an angry person again?

Do I hate Owen Brodie again?

Did I get my groove back?

...

Nope.

I want to put my mouth on his mouth and hear him tell me I'm pretty again while his love machine gets to work on me.

Shit.

19

FRANKIE

Owen Brodie has been busy. He's been busy with his shows, which Sam and I have not been attending. He's been busy doing interviews and promos and courtesy meet and greets with the local radio stations and businesses that have been sponsoring his shows. My uncle Martin did a good job of lining up sponsors for Owen and of unwittingly cock-blocking us.

Sam has always been around ever since that night in Tampa, so it's not like we would have had a chance for any more hanky-panky unless Owen snuck out of his hotel room while Sam was sleeping. And he didn't. And that's good because I didn't want him to.

I mean, it would have been nice if he'd asked so I could tell him no, but he has done a remarkable and annoying job of adhering to the stupid ground rules that I set for us in Tampa.

Now that we're heading to New York, I am composed of approximately ninety percent butterflies about this hypothetical date night that Owen proposed, and the rest is anxiety about Sam sneaking cheese into his mouth when I'm not looking.

We're in the first-class lounge, and the buffet includes a troubling amount of cheese cubes. His dad and I have both explained to him why it's important for all of us to avoid consuming large amounts of cheese before we travel, but the little bugger is sneaky. He asked if melted cheese counts. He said that we made him eat toast after he ate the pocket cheese in Tampa and he didn't have any tummy troubles. So why can't he have grilled cheese sandwiches before a flight? We didn't have any other answer other than "because we say so."

We both sound so much like his parents now, Owen and I. I could cry.

But I'm not going to think about that.

I'm just the nanny.

And only a temporary one at that.

My job as his temporary nanny mainly centers on watching dark cartoons and nature shows with him, setting up daily FaceTime calls with him and his mother, being on cheese patrol, and ensuring that he doesn't do a faceplant into anyone or anything when he takes naps in public places.

Sam has quickly become one of my all-time favorite people, and I really want him to have the cheese if he wants the cheese.

But I also really don't want to deal with cheese poops ever again in my life.

We're hanging out in a secluded area with a cluster of armchairs and a little sofa. Owen is sitting to the right of me, and Sam is to my left. I'm watching Sam watch *Batman* on his iPad with his headphones on. His red hair is really messy today, but I like it that way. He keeps looking up longingly at the buffet across the room and then glancing over at me and frowning. I'm the Cheese Nazi, and he's not happy with me this morning.

"He wasn't always obsessed with cheese," Owen says in a hushed voice. He's been reading something on his laptop for the past twenty minutes, but I guess he caught Sam's cheese yearning too. "It used to be ice cream. Before that it was bacon bits. Not bacon strips—just the bits. Before that it was chocolate cake. Before that it was chocolate milk." He sighs. "Does he seem unhappy to you?"

"No." I don't even have to think about it. "He doesn't."

"Really?"

"I think he's just super chill."

"Yeah? I mean, that's what I've always thought

177

too, but… It's good to get a second opinion. I always worry that I'm doing something wrong. The way I am with him."

I turn to face him. "Are you kidding? You're great with him. You have a seven-year-old son who isn't a people pleaser. He knows who he is, and he likes himself. And he grew up in *Los Angeles*. Do you not realize how big a deal that is?"

He smiles. "I guess."

When I turn back to look at Sam, I feel Owen's fingertips graze the back of my hand.

Just that.

The slightest touch, just for a second, and I catch my breath, my eyes snap shut, my heart starts racing, and all the energy of the world is centered in my belly.

"You're coming to the party with me tonight, right?"

Owen doesn't have a show tonight, and his brother Dylan is taking the night off from his Broadway play to look after Sam all afternoon and all night. Owen will be shooting a music video, and he asked me if I want to go watch, but I declined his offer.

I have to clear my throat. "I already told my girl-friends I'd go to dinner with them."

"Good. Come by afterward."

I want to. I really want to. But I also don't.

"What have you been reading?"

178

"Trying to change the subject, huh? Pretty smooth. They sent me the new draft of the pilot."

"Oh, how is it?"

He rubs his forehead and screws up his face and still looks handsome. "Better. It's just not funny enough. I know these family channel-type sitcoms aren't expected to be hilarious, but…"

"But why shouldn't they be?"

"I just wish we could sneak a little harmless innuendo in there."

"It's about a single dad, right? You should be able to get away with some veiled dick jokes."

"The dicks would have to be really veiled. And there's a… We decided to add this nanny character…"

This is so supremely pleasing to me, it's kind of embarrassing. "Oh did you, now?"

"She's nothing like you, but she's pretty sassy. She's a good foil for my character."

"A foil, huh? Not an antagonist?"

"Like I said, she's nothing like you."

"Well, maybe that's what's wrong with the script."

"Maybe. The guy they got to write the pilot is really good at character and structure and nailing the tone that executives want. But I want to give him a bunch of suggestions for jokes and words he can use to level up the comedy a bit. Push the envelope without really pushing it, you know?"

"Yeah. Veiled dick jokes."

"I guess. I'll start a Word doc."

I pull out my phone. "I have a Notes file with dick synonyms. I can help you with that."

"You carry dick slang around in your pocket?"

I glance over at him, and he looks like he's about to get down on one knee. Comedians are so weird.

"Come to the party with me."

"Maybe. You think you could get away with using pecker?"

An elderly, uptight New England-type couple walk by, frowning at me.

Instead of apologizing for making them hear the word *pecker*, I look right at them while saying, "Or how about dingus? Would that work?"

"I think we could get away with dingus," Owen says, typing it into his new document. He doesn't even notice the stink eyes we're getting. "Gonna have to pass on pecker though."

"Fair enough. Anything stick-based should work. Joystick, love stick, dipstick, whoopie stick, disco stick, meat stick. Oooh—tube steak!"

"I can work with all of those. Keep 'em coming."

"I always do. Philly cheesesteak. Baloney. Schnitzel. Beef whistle. Meat puppet. Meat sword. Wiener, obviously."

"Obviously. I'm pretty sure Barry Weiner would approve of a hairy wiener joke. Hot dog, sausage, kielbasa."

"Gravy maker might be pushing it, right?"

"As much as I enjoy pushing it, anything that involves tasty fluids or fluids being emitted from a sausage is probably off-limits. Meat popsicle would probably be fine, but not creamsicle."

"So spunk torpedo is out, then. Can't go wrong with dong, ding-dong, dongle, ding-a-ling. You are clearly familiar with the snake-related terms."

"Indeed I am. Lizard also works."

"Pud is cute. Like if an adolescent boy is pulling on his pud."

"I'm pretty sure we can't add a verb to it, but I will add pud to the list."

"Don't forget the nanny's honeypot, twinkle, or love box."

"Oh, I haven't been able to stop thinking about the nanny's love box, trust me," he says while typing and staring at the document. "I bet it tastes fucking delicious."

"You're breaking more than one ground rule right now, sir."

"I'm talking about the character. We don't have rules for characters, so I can tell you that the subtext for my character, when he's talking to the nanny character, is always that he is wondering what her honeypot tastes like."

"Are there any British characters? Because I love knob."

"I bet you do. I will pitch knob and see if it flies."

"Do that. You can also add the word joy to it."

"Joy knob." He types that into the document. "My character's knob is definitely a giver of joy, and I bet the nanny character knows it."

I shake my head, looking over at Sam to make sure he's still sitting next to me and not lying facefirst in the platter of cheese cubes. He still has his headphones on and appears to be having a very quiet conversation with the cartoon he's watching. He's so cute, I want to muss up his already messy hair, but I also don't want to disturb him.

His father, however, seems intent on disturbing me this morning. He leans in awfully close to look at my phone. "What else have you got in your Notes there?"

I lean away from him. "A lot. I mean I have notebooks for jokes, but I have files on my phone that are just thoughts about comedy in general. Like if I ever get a job on a writing staff, I'll have all this stuff ready to reference."

"Yeah? You'd want to do that? Write on a show?" He sounds surprised for some reason.

"Of course. Like a late-night show or something for Comedy Central. *SNL*, of course. I wouldn't say no to that show, but preferably if I could time travel back to when it was still awesome."

"Right. You want to work on a cool show." He sounds disappointed for some reason. "Well, what kind of thoughts are we talking about?"

"Just random things." I open up that file in my Notes app. "Like how the word sandwich is funny."

"Yeah, that's, like, Comedy 101."

"I know, and how words with *K* sounds are funnier than words with *S* sounds or any word with a bunch of vowels."

"Right. Like Frankie is funnier than Frances."

"And infinitely funnier than Owen."

"Except sandwich is an *S* word."

"Hey, I didn't make the rules. The word lady is much funnier than woman. If you add the word business or party to pretty much any funny noun it makes it funnier. Lady business. Cooter party."

"Pud party. Boner business. Hey, what about *schlong*? That's a funny S word."

"Ah yes. As an amendment to the *K* versus *S* rule —all Yiddish words are funny, especially terms for male genitalia."

"*Schlong* and *schvantz*."

"*Putz*." I can't stop smiling at him. It's terrible. "You've got a lot of *chutzpah* today, Mr. Brodie."

"I'm just so *verklempt* about getting to New York. Aren't you?"

"I am."

"Good. Meet me at the party tonight."

"Okay. It better not be a sausage party."

We smile at each other for about half a year before I finally manage to look away. I feel giddy, and it's so *meshuga*. No good can come of this.

Unless you count orgasms as a good thing, then *some* good can come of it.

But then it will just be bad.

Really bad. It might be the good kind of bad, but it will be very, very bad.

Sam is sitting next to me, but his headphones are off, his iPad is in his lap, and he's popping a cube of cheddar into his mouth.

He's a cheese ninja, and Owen and I have been acting like a couple of *schmucks*.

"Sam," Owen says in his Sexy Daddy Voice, "what did we say about the cheese?"

Sam slowly turns his head, a sly grin on his adorable face. "You said I can't eat a lot of it before the plane. I only had five cheeses." He stands up and pulls a slice of toast from the front pocket of his jeans. "And I'm going to eat this next. So it'll be like having a sandwich party in my tummy."

Yeah.

That's pretty funny.

20

DYLAN: *I think there's something seriously messed up with your son's digestive system. Please advise.*

DYLAN: *Seriously. SOS. I'm not sure I should let him sit on the rental furniture anymore.*

DYLAN: *Dude.*

DYLAN: *Dude.*

DYLAN: *There is some seriously fucked up shit going on in Sam's stomach right now. Literally. My girlfriend just left because she's scared of what's going to come out of him.*

DYLAN: *Fine. You're busy shooting the music video they should have cast me in. I'm texting the hot nanny.*

DYLAN: *Hey Frankie. It's Dylan Brodie. Owen's*

*younger hotter funnier more talented brother. He gave me
your number in case I can't get ahold of him. I can't get
ahold of him.*

FRANKIE: *Hey! Is everything okay?*

DYLAN: *Yes and no. The good news is there's a window
and a really powerful fan in the bathroom so the smell is
gone. The bad news is I might have to cover this entire
apartment with plastic sheets.*

FRANKIE: *Uh-oh. Did Sam eat cheese?*

DYLAN: *Affirmative. I took him to the restaurant across
from my place for lunch, and he wanted the cheese
fondue. He said it's fine since it's melted cheese with
bread.*

FRANKIE: *Um. Owen should have told you not to let
him eat more cheese today.*

DYLAN: *He neglected to tell me that. Probably on
purpose because he's an asshole. Any advice for me?*

FRANKIE: *Yes. Don't tell Sam any fart jokes for the rest
of the day. Don't make him laugh or scare him.*

DYLAN: *I just put on Ghostbusters. Is that bad?*

FRANKIE: *Only if you don't want to help him clean up
and change out of his underpants in a little bit.*

DYLAN: *But if I tell him he can't watch Ghostbusters I
won't be his favorite uncle anymore.*

FRANKIE: *I'm so sorry but I'm about to go down to a
subway station so I might not be able to text for a little
while. If you don't have any wet wipes you should order
some immediately. If you want me to come pick up Sam
tonight I will.*

DYLAN: *I mean. If I'm the reason you don't go to that party, Owen will straight up murder me. It's fine. I'll be fine. We'll be fine. Have a good night.*

DYLAN: *You owe me big time, bro. Big time.*

21

OWEN

I talked to Sam and Dylan when I was in the limo on the way here. Sam still thinks Dylan is the coolest guy he knows, and Dylan no longer cares if he's nominated for a Tony this year—he already thinks he's won World's Best Uncle. I am grateful to him for facilitating this night out for Frankie and me, but he will be insufferable for the rest of my life. Will it be worth it? Probably.

If Frankie ever shows up.

The rooftop bar that Nico and Alex chose for the wrap party is in a SoHo hotel, and as everyone keeps telling me, it's not super crowded because everyone's in the Hamptons right now. Shooting the music video on location was fun. But the best part of it, for me, was having someone to check in with throughout the day. That someone may be a sarcastic little turd, but she's a fucking delight to text with. Frankie may not be my girlfriend, but no woman has ever become such a significant part of my life so quickly.

I can't stop thinking about her, and I don't want to.

She said she was leaving the restaurant she was at with her friends in Brooklyn about forty-five minutes ago, and I keep waiting for her to text me to say she's here. I should go down and wait for her on the sidewalk. Maybe we should just go straight back to my hotel room. Fuck this date-night shit. My trouser monkey is ready to dance.

I'm on a sofa under a shade sail and patio lights—the meat in a Nico Todd–Alex Vega sandwich. I can feel Nico staring at me. If I were a chick, being stared at this intently by a hot musician would set my panties on fire, but I just find it annoying. He slaps my leg with the back of his hand. "Why do you look so anxious, man? Vega, we need to get this guy laid."

Alex leans forward so he can see Nico. "You thinkin' what I'm thinkin'?"

"This is a job for the Lazy Wingmen."

"Do not Lazy Wingman me." These smug married assholes have been doing their Lazy Wingman routine with me ever since the divorce, and it's never funny. Ever.

"Lazy Wingman it is." Vega puts his arm around my shoulder, then mutters in the general direction of a small group of women about ten feet from us. They're looking the other way and definitely can't hear him over the music. "Hey. Check out this dude. He's a man. With a penis. He's got a pair of really manly, well-groomed eyebrows. He also has a job. What do you think? You want some of that?"

"I got this, I got this." Nico raises his chin at a woman who's deep in conversation with a guy at a table across from us. "Yo, baby, what's up? I see you lookin' at my friend over here. Oh, you're looking at *me*? I get it. But I'm taken. This guy, though. He's here. He's alive. He'll probably buy you a drink or something. You should give him a chance."

These guys are really cracking each other up.

"Okay." I polish off my drink. "That was hilarious."

Alex looks down at his phone while waving at no one in particular. "Hang on, ladies. Anyone want a piece of this guy over here? He comes with a lot of unisex hair products. He smells like a leather jacket that got left out on a tropical beach and then some exotic jungle animal peed on it. He's not the worst guy here, so y'know. You should talk to him or whatever."

"I got it, I got it." Nico addresses a very drunk girl who is holding on to one of her girlfriends for support and has her eyes closed. "Hey. You look like you're having trouble standing up. This guy right here has a hotel room somewhere. Whaddya say?"

"Are you done?"

"Take your pick, dude. We got 'em lined up for you." Alex pats me on the knee.

"Thanks, but I'm actually not looking."

Nico studies me skeptically. "Oh yeah? Because you seem to be looking for *someone*."

"So there's someone in particular you need us to wingman for you?" Alex asks.

"There is absolutely no one I need you to wingman for me. You're a great director and a terrible friend."

"I'm fine with that."

"Hey, what about me?" Nico whines. He even makes whining sound sexy.

"You are a very talented singer-songwriter slash musician and I sort of want to lick your face, but you are also a shitty friend."

"I *would* let you lick my face though. Who's the someone in particular?"

I'm already grinning just thinking about her, and it's so lame. "Officially, there is no one in particular. Unofficially, there's a particular someone who's meeting me here. Someone from LA who's been traveling with Sam and me."

Nico frowns at me. "You mean because you're paying her to?"

Alex scrubs his face and affects total agony. "Not the nanny. Please tell me you haven't fallen for a hot nanny."

191

Bunch of hypocrites. Nico fell for the woman he paid to go on tour with him as his photographer. Alex fell for his son's teacher.

I shake my head, glancing over at the open glass doors from the interior of the bar to the terrace, and I don't even care about defending myself to these guys anymore.

I don't remember to breathe.

I don't see or hear one other person in this city right now.

Because Frankie Hogan has arrived and she's wearing a red dress.

I'm up off the sofa, weaving through the crowd between us, and I will live in this space and time where she spots me coming toward her and smiles.

She smiles before realizing she shouldn't.

She smiles even when I can tell she's trying not to.

I walk right up to her and put my hands on her face and kiss her.

She's still smiling when I pull away, and I'm still touching her face.

"Hi. You look so pretty I want to punch something."

She laughs, and the lighting's too dim for me to tell if she's blushing but I bet she is. She's still smiling when she says, "Thank you. You look so handsome I want to throw you off this roof."

"Thanks for wearing a dress for me."

She clears her throat. "I wore the dress for New York."

"You wore it for me."

Eye-roll. "Yeah. But get over yourself."

"I'm pretty sure you're discovering how impossible it is to get over me."

And there goes the smile.

Which means it's true.

I put my arm around her waist, kissing her cheek. "I'm not getting over you either." I start to lead her toward my friends.

"Owen, I don't think we should—"

"I don't think we should either, but we're not going to think right now."

She nods.

I lean in and say into her ear, "You're not the nanny tonight, okay? You're just the only woman I want to be with."

I'm glad I have my arm around her because I feel her knees give out a little bit.

It's the first of many times I plan to make her feel lightheaded this evening.

I introduce her to Nico and Alex, a few of the crew members who are around, but then I take her over to the edge of the terrace so she can see the view. I stand behind her, wrap my arms around her waist, and kiss the top of her head. "One day, all this will be yours."

She barks out a laugh. "I'll take it."

"I mean it. You deserve it."

She places her hands over mine. "Are you going to be nice to me all night?"

"Yes."

"I don't know if I can handle it."

"I don't give a fuck. This is what you're getting. You want something from the bar?"

"Um. No. I had wine with dinner. I don't want to drink too much tonight."

"So you can remember it?"

"Don't laugh at me."

"I'm not laughing at you, Frankie. I'm gonna give you a night you'll want to remember." I take her hand and guide her back toward the interior of the bar. "Come dance with me."

She hesitates, like I knew she would.

Then she follows my lead, like I was hoping she would.

22

FRANKIE

Shit.

Owen Brodie is a good dancer, and I am so screwed.

I was screwed when he kept checking in with me all day.

I was screwed when I saw him in that tight black T-shirt that hugs his biceps and pecs.

I was screwed when he was staring at me in my red dress.

I was screwed when he touched my face and kissed me even before saying hello.

I was screwed every time he said every single thing he's said since I got here.

And now I am so, so screwed. Because we're dancing to some sexy mid-tempo song that I don't know, in this tiny crowded space between the bar and the seating area, and he doesn't move like a tired dad who hasn't been out on a date for ages and just needs to get some. He moves like a man who knows what he wants. And he wants me.

I am so, so, so screwed because I want him more than I've ever wanted anyone or anything—more than I want to make people laugh, even. I didn't think I'd ever want anything more than I want that. And I don't know how to stop wanting him. I can't even pretend that I don't want him anymore. I don't even want to pretend.

This is the worst fucking thing that's ever happened to me.

I don't know how I can be so scared of someone who makes me feel this good, but I'm terrified.

All I can do is breathe and move my feet and sway my hips and shoulders and try so hard not to fall that I forget how to breathe and keep moving when this is all over. Whether it's over in the morning or in August. Or whenever. Because it's more than one boy I'm falling in love with here.

I had no trouble giving all of myself to Sam as soon as I met him, but I will always worry that if I give too much to his dad, I won't get it back.

I don't think I can turn this into a joke, and I certainly don't want to be the punchline.

Owen is watching me as if he can read my every thought. His electric-blue eyes are warm, and I can't look away. "Hey." He curls his index finger beneath my chin, tilting it up so he can kiss my lips, quick and easy. As if to say, *Get out of your head, Frankie Hogan. This is supposed to be fun.*

He's right.

If I just concentrate on the way he's moving and the way he's looking at me and the tingles in my lady business, I'm fine.

More than fine.

More than anything.

I run my fingers through my hair and sway my shoulders and my hips a little more. He does the same. He puts his hands on my hips, and I grip his shirt with both hands. I move in closer until I can feel it on my thigh—how aroused he is. I want to touch him there, with my hands, but it can wait.

"You want to get out of here?" His voice is deeper now, and I can feel it even more than I can feel the bassline of this music in my bones.

"Yeah. I want to."

He texts "the driver" to ask him to come pick us up. He texts his gorgeous celebrity friends while we're waiting for the elevator, instead of finding them to say goodbye. He texts Dylan to make sure Sam's doing okay. As soon as he gets Dylan's response telling him that Sam's doing great, Owen is clearly as relieved as I am tense because this means it will probably be just him and me until we go meet up with them for brunch tomorrow.

Hours and hours and inches and inches of him and me.

I'm already quivering.

And I can't tell if I'm more worried that it will be too much for me to handle or not nearly enough.

We're alone in the elevator all the way down to the lobby, and we kiss the whole time. It's not frantic kissing like in Tampa. It's *this is going to last all night* kissing, like grown-ups who know what they're doing. I've never thought of myself as one of those before, but I feel like one now. Owen Brodie's lips and tongue and hands and that stiff, wonderful thing in his pants, they're all making me feel like the grown-up woman I never knew I could be.

"You are so fucking gorgeous in this red dress, Frankie."

I try to think of some witty reply, but I can't. So I just say, "Thank you." And I mean it.

"I can't take my eyes off you."

"Good."

It's warmer and more humid out here on the sidewalk, or maybe I'm warmer and more damp after that long, slow kiss, but I like it.

The New York summer night air is balmy and sultry, and it only smells a little bit like sewer and garbage. Owen keeps his arm around my waist, and I feel so safe with him. Even earlier today when I was by myself or with my girlfriends in Brooklyn, I just felt so much safer than I usually do when I'm out and about in the world. I didn't realize it until just now, but it was because I knew Owen cared about me.

Talk about cheese.

I don't even recognize my own thoughts anymore.

He gives my waist a little reassuring squeeze. He can probably tell I'm all up in my head again. A black stretch limousine with tinted windows pulls over and double-parks in front of us. I'm expecting Jay-Z and Beyoncé to climb out of it or maybe one of the Olsen twins. Instead, Owen pulls me over to it and takes hold of the door handle.

"Wait. What?"

"This is us."

"Oh fuck off. You got a limo?"

"Technically, my manager got a limo."

I like how he said "my manager" instead of "your uncle." Not that I've forgotten who his manager is. Not that that's going to stop either of us from doing whatever it is we're about to do tonight.

He opens the door to the back seat, leans in to tell the driver he doesn't have to get out, and then gestures for me to climb aboard. "Milady."

I peer inside first to ensure there isn't some reality show camera crew in there waiting to record my reaction.

There isn't.

So I have to get in.

I haven't been inside a limo since prom. That one

was white, and my date and I shared it with six other grads. This is nothing like that.

I slide down to the rear seat and scan the interior.

Dark-gray leather, blue LED lighting, sleek bar setup, glossy wood paneling, flat screen TV, privacy window between us and the driver... Do I want to stand up and stick my head through the sunroof like Tom Hanks in *Big*? Yes, indeedy, I do. But this is not that kind of date, unfortunately.

Owen settles in right next to me. "Will you relax, Hogan?"

"Nope. I don't think I've even been on a date with a guy who wears a belt before—how am I supposed to relax in the back of a limo?"

"I have some pretty good ideas." He presses the button on an intercom, waits for the driver to answer, and tells him he can take his time getting us back to the hotel. Head up to Central Park and drive around, he tells him—and keep the privacy barrier up, if he doesn't mind.

I know what *that* means.

We slowly pull into traffic, and I squeeze my thighs together because *Dear Lord* things are getting tight and wet up in there. Owen fiddles with some controls on the stereo system. When he finds a satellite station he likes—I dunno, I guess there's a special one for Limo Nookie—he leans back against the seat.

He doesn't look at me. He just removes my shoes

and then places his hand on my bare leg, just above the knee. He strokes a tiny section of my skin so gently, but I feel it intensely, everywhere. Then he angles himself toward me, touches my face with his other hand, bringing me in for a kiss. He lifts the backs of my knees to rest my legs on his lap, and my hand goes straight for the crotch of his pants. I make no pretense of being a lady, and *wow* I love how hard he's getting, even though he seems so cool and in control.

I'm so used to being the performer when I'm with a guy. Always felt like I had to put on a show of passion and satisfaction. But I trust that Owen is going to make me feel all the things he wants to make me feel, and I think for now I'm just going to let him do it.

I curl up in his arms. His breathing gets heavier, his kisses more and more urgent. Still, his hand travels slowly up the side of me—my leg, my hip, my waist. Any resistance I had left in my body and my mind is gone. Just gone.

He trails kisses down my neck and my chest until his mouth meets his hand on my breast, and *Oh God* it feels so good, I gasp.

"I've been thinking about these tits for days," he growls as he tests the low neckline of my dress to see if the material stretches, and *Hallefuckinlujah* it does! He pulls it down, exposing my nipple because I'm not wearing a bra. He grunts, staring down at it. "So fucking hot, Frankie." He licks me once and then squeezes. "You have no idea what you do to me, do you?"

Oh my, I guess it's time for the dirty-talk portion of the evening.

"Tell me."

"You feel how hard I am?"

"Yes."

"Nobody gets me this hard but you." He kisses me all over my breast, licking and sucking, and I'm already so close to orgasm I want to cry.

"Yeah?"

"Yeah." His hand slides down my thigh and then up under my dress. "Whatcha got for me under here?" His fingers slip inside my panties, and he groans when he feels how wet I am, like he's in pain. "Fucking hell, baby. You really like me, don't you?"

"I like you a lot right now."

"You do, huh?" He maneuvers me so my back lies flat on the seat and yanks my panties down, startling me. He bends one of my legs to the side of him and holds the other one up, kissing me from my ankle— slowly, agonizingly slowly—down to my inner thigh. "I'm gonna make you feel so good, you won't remember what it was like to hate me."

"Big talker," I mumble, staring up at the ceiling.

"What was that?" He slaps my ass.

"It's going to take a lot to get me to forget how much I hated you, is all I'm saying." God, I'm sassy. I don't know where I get the strength, but I had to throw one more taunt out there before I start chanting his name and dissolving into a pool of lady fluids.

He curls his arms around my thighs, tilts, and opens me up, and I hear him mutter, "You asked for it," before flicking his tongue at my clit and then circling it.

I reach back for something to grab on to—because I'm gonna need it.

I'm wriggling around so much. I'm not a scientist or anything, but I'm probably creating so much friction between the inside of my thighs and his ears, it will produce a flame. Owen struggles to hold me in place so he can control what he's doing. I have never felt so out of control in my life, and—surprise, surprise—*I love it*.

He does all the things I always wished a guy would do down there. The thumb thing. The warm breath thing. The guttural-sounds-that-create-vibrations thing. The tongue-fucking thing. He pauses, pulls his head back to kiss the inside of my thigh again—because he's evil or because he's a genius. The delirious shuddering and trembling had no beginning, and it seems there will be no end to this exquisite torture. He stops kissing me altogether, and now he's just making me wait.

My hands find the top of his head and tug at his hair. "Owen," I plead.

"You want more?"

"Yes."

"You sure you're ready? I don't think your pussy can take much more of this."

My hands curl into fists, and I punch the back of the seat with one of them. "I am so mad at you."

I swear like a marine as I try to sit up, but he forces me back down, flips the skirt of my dress up, and just goes to town French-kissing the most tender part of me until I cry out. No words, just pure anguish and pleasure. My body moves with his head and his tongue. I have never said *yes* so many times in a row in my life, and I have no idea if the limo is moving or what neighborhood we're in, but there's so much dropping and rolling and tumbling going on below my belly button. There's a jolt of electricity, and my back arches. I'm suspended in time and place for who knows how long, until I'm dropping and rolling and tumbling again.

Owen doesn't stop.

No, I keep saying. I can't take any more of this, my brain is telling me.

But my body wants more, and this man seems to know exactly what my body wants.

Suddenly, his head pulls out from between my legs. He flips me around and maneuvers me so I'm sitting up with my hands against the window, one foot on the floor. He slides under me like a fucking acrobat, grips my ass with both hands, and pulls me down so he can suck on my clit—which is just mean. I make a high-pitched yelping sound, and then his tongue goes deep inside me. In and out and in and out.

It's too much.

I don't ever want him to stop, but it's too much.

If anyone had told me a month ago that I would be riding Owen Brodie's face in the back of a limo in New York City, I would have slapped them and told them to shut up.

But this is happening.

I will have to retire the red dress and maybe my vagina too after tonight because no experience can possibly top this.

The palms of my hands are pressing so hard against the window, I'm afraid we'll both crack from the pressure.

It's like all the energy that powers this city is concentrated in my abdomen, and now it's being released to every cell in my body.

I can't even make a sound.

He keeps kissing me there until I go limp.

I lift myself up, lie down on top of him, the side of my face flat against his pec. His heart is pounding. His jaw must be so sore. I want to return the favor, but I think it will have to wait until we get to the hotel room.

When I'm finally able to lift my head up enough to see his face, I find him looking down at me, grinning. His eyes are hooded and blurry, and I've never found them so beautiful. He slowly wipes his mouth with the back of his hand, holding my gaze, and then dips down to kiss my forehead.

"Got any notes for me?"

It's not funny, but I laugh and bury my face in his chest.

I'll get him back, but I will let him have this moment of glory.

"Congratulations. You killed," I mumble.

And then I wrap my arms around his waist and fall asleep.

23

OWEN

When you make a lady come on your face, you earn yourself the right to smirk and act all cocky with said lady for at least a full hour afterward, no matter where you are or what you're doing.

When you make a lady come on your face in a limo, you earn yourself the right to play the theme from *Rocky* on your phone while you and your lady friend stand up through the sunroof with your arms in the air as you cruise down Central Park West. In addition, it earns you the right to high-five your chauffeur and random strangers in a hotel lobby as well as sing "Pussy Monster" by Lil Wayne in the elevator up to your floor, making your lady blush and shake her head at you while trying so very hard not to laugh.

When you make your son's hot nanny, who is also your manager's niece and the only woman you've had any feelings for in years, come on your face in a limo and then she asks if it's okay for her to go to her room to freshen up before joining you in yours—you say yes. Of course you do. We've got all night. Nothing wrong with a little interlude for freshening up and gathering strength and hydrating and whatnot. But if a few minutes becomes fifteen or twenty minutes and she's not replying to your texts—no amount of sexual confidence can prevent you from wondering if she's having regrets and doubts. Perhaps she spoke to your ex-wife and got a concise list of your flaws as a romantic partner, and maybe—*shit, what if she was faking the orgasms just to be nice?*

That last thing is basically impossible, and the way things were with my ex-wife aren't relevant, but Frankie wouldn't be wrong to question whether or not we should do this. Of course we shouldn't. But this is one of those rare situations in life where you really have to do the thing you shouldn't do because it's the *this is wrong* part that will make it so, so right. No one's cheating on anyone here. We're both adults here. We're two very hot and horny single adults who need to do the thing that they shouldn't do before one of their tortured big, hard cocks falls off.

When you finally hear that familiar quiet-yet-determined knock on the door to your suite, it is totally natural for your heart to start racing and very cool of you to fist pump and whisper "*yessss*" before opening the door.

One might expect a young woman such as Frankie Hogan to appear at a hotel room door wearing a trench coat and heels—to casually sway her hips as she enters while slowly removing her trench coat to reveal some super-classy-yet-equally-naughty lingerie underneath it.

But somehow, even when you find her standing there in Snoopy pajamas with a nervous expression on her naked face, you find her sexy and endearing and altogether likable. Lovable, even. And totally fuckable.

"Hi. I was about to go over and check on you." I take her hand and lead her inside, feeling a little overdressed.

"I got nervous."

When you're a professional comedian, you do get a sense of when a joke is going to fall flat, but I decide to say this anyway: "Is this your first time? I'll be gentle."

I don't get a laugh.

She squeezes my hand and looks up at me, sighing. "Please tell me you're terrible at *schtupping*."

"Sorry, baby. That's just not the feedback I've gotten."

She rests her forehead against my chest. "Don't say we're doing this to get it out of our systems, okay?" She sounds so vulnerable all of a sudden.

I wrap my arms around her.

I want to build her a house and carry her around in my arms all the time and sing her a lullaby or something.

But I also want to schtup her.

She takes a breath and continues, "If we do this now, I'm going to give you everything. Even if it doesn't last."

I knew it. I knew she was a romantic. I knew it.

"I want your everything, Frankie. Even if it's just a bottomless pit of sarcasm and veiled dick jokes. And I've been waiting to give you everything ever since you mauled me in Tampa."

I get smacked in the arm for that, and rightly so. She offered me three rare jewels of genuine sentences, and I gave her one and a half asshole replies.

"What I mean is..."

Before I can finish that sentence, she says, "Saying you're going to have sex with someone you're really attracted to so you can get it out of your system is like going to Target and saying you're just going to buy *one* thing."

"Trying out jokes before we schtup for the first time, huh? I like it. That's a good one."

"It's mine. I call dibs on the Target joke."

"You can have it. I call dibs on *you*."

"You can have me. Grab a cart because I have a lot to offer."

"I'm getting two carts because I'm going to grab everything."

I grab her ass, pick her up.

The sound she makes at the back of her throat is caught somewhere between a gasp and a moan, but it's hot as hell.

Her legs wrap around my waist, and I carry her over to the dresser, placing her on top of it.

I lean in to kiss her, but she pulls my shirt off over my head and then pulls the Snoopy shirt off over hers.

I do a full-on doubletake because it's like a fucking mirage.

She's wearing a fancy, black lacy bra thing that pushes her tits up, and I want my hands and mouth all over them.

But I keep my cool.

"Well, now. What have we here?"

She's grinning at me—little minx. "You like? Because there's more where that came from, if you're interested." She points down at the area below her waist.

"I'm moderately to extremely interested and intrigued."

She places her palms flat against the top of the dresser, hiking herself up, so I can yank those Snoopy pajama bottoms down. They drop to the floor, and now I want to drop to one knee because this woman came to my hotel room wearing some

211

kind of French lingerie getup under Snoopy pajamas. There's a thing around her waist with dainty
suspenders attached to black stockings, and *fuck me
running through Target with two carts* I don't even
know where to start.

"What are you—what—what is this—why—why
why why why are you so fucking hot, you monster?"

She leans back, rests her foot on my chest, and
drags her fingers over one breast, down her waist
and the top of her thigh to the little gold buckle at
the end of the strap holding the stockings up.

"I've never worn this for anyone before." Her
voice is all sex kitten-y all of a sudden. "Do you
know how to take these off?" She bites her lower lip
and bats her eyelashes at me.

I hold her gaze and have both of those things
unbuckled and the stockings pulled off her legs
before she even realizes what's happening.

I expect that to piss her off. Instead, she looks
nervous again. Did she not expect me to be so
competent at removing ladies' undergarments?
Sorry, honey. I got this.

I stare into those big brown eyes as I reach
between her legs, slipping my fingers inside those
fancy lace panties, and what I find in there is so
simple and just pure, heavenly Frankie. Her clit is
slick and warm, and I take my time reacquainting
myself with her. It's only been about an hour since
my tongue was down there, but she's responding to

my touch like it's the first time. Shivering and trembling. She is somehow simultaneously receptive and resistant, and it's so fucking sexy.

What kind of idiot would I have to be to think I could get enough of her in one night?

She whimpers. Arches her back because I know she wants me to pay attention to those tits, and I plan to. She pouts and leans forward to kiss me, but I pull back. She's so aroused she can't even get mad at me, and I can tell that *that* makes her mad too. And more aroused.

She wriggles around, chest heaving, eyes shut, head falls back.

She is right on the edge, and now is the time for my fingers to leave that slippery pearl and tend to other parts of her.

She makes that gasp-y, moan-y sound again, opens her eyes—glares at me.

Oh, she's mad.

Good.

She continues to glare at me, squeezing her thighs together when I reach around to unhook her bra. As soon as the tension is released, the arm straps fall and those glorious tits spill forth, and this...this is so much more beautiful than what I'd imagined. I'm just staring.

She slips her arms through the straps, tosses the bra aside, and makes a move to punch my bicep. I grab that wrist. Grab her other wrist and hold her arms behind her back, dipping down to take one perfect nipple into my mouth.

"You are such an asshole," she whispers.

She's breathing so hard.

"Do you have notes for me, Tampa Heckler?"

She tenses up and says, "Yes. Enough with the edging. Just fuck me on the bed right now."

One more swirl and lick with my tongue, and then I release her wrists. "I can do that."

I carry her to the bed, drop her from just high enough so I can watch her bounce magnificently on the mattress.

She frowns at me as she sits up, unbuckles my belt, undoes my pants, and takes great care in removing my tortured big, hard cock from the boxer briefs that could barely contain it. She cups my balls, holds the base with the other hand, and mutters, "Sonofabitch," as she licks and sucks and strokes, just enough to punish me for edging her and just enough to reward me for what I did in the limo. She licks up the shaft one last time, kisses the tip, and then looks up at me.

She's waiting for me to get a condom. I retrieve the package, which she takes from me, again being very careful as she rolls it on—and I want to build that house for her again. She may be nervous, but she is also very competent and very, very thoughtful.

She takes off her fancy panties, pulls down the lacy thing that was around her waist. I watch her crawl backward to the head of the bed. Totally naked and completely stunning.

I can't get in there fast enough.

Hovering over her, I ask, "You ready for me?"

"You're joking, right?"

"Darlin', when it comes to this particular act, I am very serious."

She sucks in a breath, stares down at me where I'm positioned right there at her entrance, and nods.

She bends her legs as soon as I push in. I go slow because her pussy is deliciously tight and deliriously wet, but she releases the most impressive string of swear words, and goddammit, it's so hot. "I did ask if you were ready, milady."

"I'm fine." Her voice is low and shaky. "It feels so fucking good I want to punch your face. But get over yourself."

It does feel so fucking good. So much tension, so smooth, and a perfect fit. It feels like Frankie and me. It feels like the kind of home I'll always be excited and comfortable in and always want to come back to.

She hisses, makes a high-pitched sigh, and I groan when I'm in as deep as I can go.

Some single dad part of me just wants to make sweet, slow love to this woman so she knows exactly how much she means to me.

That part is completely overtaken by the part of me that wants to jungle fuck her until she screams my name and I can't remember who I am other than the man who gets to fuck Frankie Hogan.

She wraps her legs around mine, giving me a little nudge to let me know that I can start moving now.

And I do.

I thrust hard and fast because I know she can take it.

Her fingernails scrape down my back and it stings and I like it and it spurs me on in the way that only she can.

I get up on my knees, staying inside her, lift her up by her hips so she's arching back. Her arms hang above her head, and I watch her tits bounce around while I thrust at her G-spot. She practically starts singing. She keeps her waist up like a good girl so I can ram into her, and just when I think she couldn't be any hotter, she starts caressing herself. It's so fucking beautiful. I could watch her all night.

But I also can't.

I lean forward, going deeper.

She cries out a *yes, oh shit, fuck, yes*, reaching back to place her hands on the headboard so she can push back onto me.

"Frankie. Fuck."

She screams my name, just like I need her to.

I'm so close.

I lower her back down to the mattress so I can ride high and drill into her. She starts jerking and thrashing around because I'm stimulating her clit with my cock and there's so much friction between us. Her eyes are shut tight, her mouth a perfect O, and then a bead of my sweat drops onto her forehead. She opens her eyes and we stare at each other, and I have never even wanted to stare into a woman's eyes while fucking her before but it's so intense. We both try to keep our eyes open as long as we can, but mine snap shut when I come. And I come like a rocket. I know she's coming at the same time, and that has never happened to me before either.

There is no "before."

There's no women before Frankie, no Justins before me.

No jobs or uncles or kids to worry about.

No banter or jokes.

There's just my body and hers. And the incredible power of that friction between us. And the unbearable joy and pain that's left when we're completely still and connected to each other like this.

When we finally exhale and I lower myself to lie on top of her, I kiss her cheek and wrap my arms around her waist.

Maybe I pass out for a bit.

When I wake up, I can hear her sniffling.

I raise my head so I can see her face.

"Are you crying?"

She swipes at her cheekbone. "Shut up." The smirk and the gentle manner in which she strokes my back is in direct opposition to the way she deadpans, "Exactly how long of a refractory period do you have? Because I'm going to give you one or two chances to redeem yourself tonight. I think you can do better."

Lady Hilarious McFunnyPants just earned herself a little smack on the ass, ladies and gentlemen.

I feel something stirring already.

On with the show.

FRANKIE

So this is what it's like to *not* be cloaked in regret or disappointment after having intercourse with someone. After having totally pleasurable, relatively sober, emotionally significant, somewhat acrobatic coitus. Three times in a row.

I wonder if I can write a song about this that's still funny.

What rhymes with multiple orgasms?…

Erotic muscle spasms.

Lovable sarcasm.

Combustible enthusiasm.

These are all phrases that are totally applicable to our relationship.

"Are you writing jokes in your head?" Owen returns from the bathroom in his black boxer briefs, with his skin that's exfoliated and moisturized from head to toe, and that *I told you I was good at sex* expression on his face that doesn't even make me mad.

"You don't know me!" I reach for my phone and email those words that rhyme with multiple orgasms to myself so I don't forget them. "Yeah. Sort of."

He reunites with me under the covers, and it just feels so right, wearing Snoopy pajamas and being in the same bed with him. "You emailing yourself?"

"Yes. Do you do that?"

"Yeah. I always wake up in the middle of the night and email myself, and then when I read my messages in the morning, I usually email myself back and I'm like, *the fuck were you thinking, idiot?*"

I put the phone back onto the side table and flip around to face him. We're both propped up on an elbow, gazing at each other. If I didn't like us so much right now, I'd puke because we're so cute it's gross. "Do you ever worry you'll stop thinking like a comedian if you're really happy?"

"Like right now, you mean?" He grins at me.

My insides turn to mush. My skin is all prickly. I can't look at him when he's all sex-hair and satisfaction and making googly eyes at me. *Who even is this guy?*

Shit, I can't even think in proper English anymore.

He touches my chin, turning my head back to face him. "Don't you look away from me, missy. I am really happy right now. So are you. But we can go back to talking shit with each other for a while if that would make you feel better."

I sit up and clasp my hands in front of my heart. "Could we really?! I would like that very much."

"Course you would. You're an asshole."

"Right back atcha, asshole. This feels better. Good idea, asshole."

"You want to go out and grab a bite, asshole?"

"Now? It's after midnight!"

"Yeah. We're in the city that never sleeps, you lame-ass, ancient asshole."

"Oh man, I can't wait to be old so people will stop asking me if I want to go out. Can't we just have something from the minibar?"

"Yes, Grandma Hogan. We shall dine on the finest Pringles and Toblerone."

"Stop talking dirty to me."

"I can't help it if everything I say turns you on."

He's right, dammit, and he knows it.

I am so turned on just from watching him remove items from the minibar in his boxer briefs. This is the kind of porn I would want to watch. Hot guys in their underpants fetching sweet-and-salty snacks post-coitally while being witty.

I need to change the subject, fast.

"I think I'll be a really terrific old person."

"Don't underestimate yourself. I think you're pretty great at it now."

I toss a pillow at him. "I'm four years younger than you."

"Yes, but I take better care of my skin, and who uses the word *terrific* unironically if they're under seventy?"

"Oh my God, I wish I was seventy. I can't wait to complain about my sciatica and make strangers uncomfortable by telling them about my urinary incontinence and what a peach I was *in my day*."

He shuts the minifridge door with his foot and carries an armful of treats over to the bed. I flatten the covers so he can spread it all out for us. If he suggests ordering a pizza, I might ask him to marry me.

"Oh, you're doing a bit. It's cute. What's your lead-in? Just the 'I think I'll be a really terrific old person' thing?"

I grab the bag of peanut M&Ms when he goes back for bottled waters.

"Do you really want to know?"

"I don't ask questions that I don't want to know the answers to."

"Wow. What's it like to be a next-level grownup?"

"Sucks. What's it like to be a sarcastic asshole all the time?"

"It's fucking amazing. I don't know why everyone isn't like this."

He places two bottled waters on the bedside

table, climbs under the covers with me, and it feels so right I want to weep.

"Just tell me the bit."

"Well, I was going to open with: How's it going for you guys? Are you winning at life? Because I've been thinking lately that I peaked in day care. I was so good at taking naps when I was told to and eating pieces of fruit and sniffing glue in the bathroom…"

He considers this for a moment before declaring, "That is not good."

"Yeah. I know. Which part—all of it?"

"The first two lines are cute, and then it nose-dives. I mean I like the shape of it."

"Stop saying my stuff is cute."

"Being cute is part of your act."

"No. It's not."

"Yeah." He pats my leg. "It is."

"That's so condescending."

"I'm not being condescending. You're just reacting to what I'm saying by being insulted. That's not my fault."

I huff. I huff around him a lot. He probably thinks it's cute.

"Being cute is part of Seinfeld's act too. It's not just a girl thing."

"You aren't seriously comparing me to Jerry Seinfeld right now, are you?"

"No, I'm not comparing you to him—he's a legendary comedian whose act is widely-appreciated and pretty timeless. You're a super-hot and very talented fledgling comedian. That's a fact. I'm saying part of his act is sharing his cute thoughts. Part of your act is being cute."

He's right. I hate that he's right. But he is right. "I guess."

"You know what, I guess that bit's not so bad. Keep going with it."

"No, it's lame. I'm not doing stand-up anymore anyway."

"Yeah, that's not a thing. Quitting stand-up isn't a thing."

"Yeah. I know."

"It sucks."

"Yeah. It does."

"But we persevere. Because we're lucky we know what we want." He looks at me meaningfully. I hope I know what he's thinking because I'm thinking something so corny right now. Thank God we don't have to say it out loud.

I want you. Do you still want me too?

"You want to watch a movie or something, Golden Girl?" He gets the TV remote. "Or are you going to fall asleep soon?"

"Yeah. Let's watch a movie or something. Maybe a sitcom so I don't have to commit to staying awake."

I sample all of the snacks while he scrolls through the hotel's onscreen offerings.

"Oooh! *Seinfeld*!" I blurt out. "Since we were just

speaking of him. You ever watch it with the sound off and make up your own filthy dialogue? I do that with my roommate when we're hungover. It's really fun."

"I am definitely down for that. Which episode?"

"Doesn't matter. Click on anything."

He selects an episode, hits the Mute button, swipes the Pringle container from me, and sits back against the headboard. "You leave any for me?"

"Uh-huh." I somehow manage to tear my gaze away from the general area between Owen Brodie's lower abdominal region and his upper thighs so I can watch Jerry Seinfeld talk into a microphone. Jerry is wearing a brown suit and tie. There is something wrong with my priorities, but there is also something incredibly satisfying about putting dirty words into the smiling mouth of the cleanest comedian. "Welcome to the Thunderdome," I say in my best Seinfeld impression. "I have a giant erection in my pants, and you're all dirty sluts. Who wants a piece of me?"

I think this is the bit where Seinfeld is talking about bumper car rides, which is great because he's miming driving a little bumper car and waving his arm around yelling at someone.

"You know when you're drilling a chick from behind in the bathroom stall at a bus station, and all of a sudden you can't remember if you turned off the stove when you left home?" Owen's Seinfeld impression might be better than mine, and that actually pisses me off a little bit.

Not to be outdone, I add, "And you have to ramp things up but she just won't squontch, and you're like, *Come onnnnnnn!*"

"Come on my big, hard cock so I can call my housekeeper and ask her to go to my mansion and check the stove, you smexy ho muffin!"

"What is the deal with women who take forever to drop a load on your fuck truck?"

Jerry keeps waving his hand around, shaking his head and smiling while he talks.

"This is why you should never bang hos you meet in bus stations!" Owen declares.

"Or why you should always check the stove before leaving the house to bang hos in bus stations."

Seinfeld starts turning around in circles while miming holding a bumper car wheel. Owen is laughing too hard to speak anymore, so I yell out, "Finally, she starts spinning around on your bonedaddy like a Cirque du Soleil acrobat, and you're like, 'Attention passengers, the Red Line to Jizzville will be arriving at the station in three... two...onnnnnnneuhhhhhhh.'"

And that's the end of the opening credits sequence.

Owen is laughing so hard he can't make a sound or move. His hands are resting on his totally flat belly. He's probably growing two more abs right now because he's just hovering there mid-crunch.

The gang is in a booth at the coffee shop, and Kramer is yammering, so I just keep going. "Okay, you can take the F Train to Poundtown and then transfer to the Number 69 at Porkington Cross-roads, but make sure you don't get off until your dick diva's reached the end of the line."

Owen grabs me and pulls me to him for a kiss. "Stop. I can't take it anymore."

"I win!"

"I didn't know it was a competition, but sure. You win. You have a filthy, magnificent mouth."

"Thank you."

His sapphire-blue eyes are all glossy and glittery, and I actually feel like I'm winning at life for once.

"Hey." He strokes my arm with his fingertip, and it sends shivers down my everything, everywhere. "Are you still hungry? Should we order a pizza?"

Shit.

I am so deliriously happy right now.

Yes.

I want to eat pizza with this man and his son for the rest of my life, I think.

"Why do you look like you're gonna cry? We don't have to order pizza. It was just a suggestion."

I attach my mouth to his because the thing that I want to say to him is no joke and I've been on a roll and I'm just not willing to risk bombing at the high point of the night.

25

FRANKIE: *Heyyyyy! How's it going?!*

MIA: *OMG you had sex with him didn't you?!?!?! <partying face emoji> It was great wasn't it? Tell me everything.*

FRANKIE: *Um. There were mouths and hands and there was bare skin and a penis and a vagina involved but other than that it was unlike anything I've ever experienced and he's ruined my life. I'm so mad at him but I can't feel mad at him anymore because my body is so happy so that just makes my brain want to be even more mad at him. But it can't. If that makes sense.*

MIA: *It makes sense for you, yes. Awww, Frankie. I'm so happy. I knew you liked him. I knew his winky-face emoticon meant something.*

FRANKIE: *<neutral face emoji>*

MIA: *<smiling face with three hearts emoji>*

FRANKIE: *I'm terrified. And I don't know why. It's so dumb.*

MIA: *You're falling in love for the first time. It's nice.*

FRANKIE: *It's the worst thing I've ever experienced. I hate it.*

MIA: *I'm so happy for you.*

FRANKIE: *Stop saying that! It's making my skin crawl.*

FRANKIE: *But thank you. Love you. You're a really good friend. And all that other stuff that nice people say to other nice people IDK just thank you for always being so supportive.*

MIA: *OMG who are you?! You must have had SO many orgasms.*

FRANKIE: *Basically still having them. But I'm still terrified.*

MILES: *Nice going, Casanova. I hear you banged the hot nanny. Way to take the wrong brother's advice.*

OWEN: *Trust me, I wasn't taking Dylan's advice, and thanks for your discretion, dickhead.*

DYLAN: *I was explaining to him how awesome I was with Sam, and he guessed the nanny-banging part, twatface.*

OWEN: *Let's not refer to her as that and let's not refer to the act we engaged in multiple amazing times as that.*

MILES: *Sorry. I hear you made sweet love to the hot lady you're paying to look after your child who's also a come-*

*dian who also happens to be your manager's favorite
niece.*

OWEN: *Shit. Did he say she's his favorite?*

MILES: *I think she's his only niece.*

OWEN: *Shit.*

DYLAN: *Nice going, spunktrumpet.*

MILES: *Good one.*

DYLAN: *Sir Patrick Stewart has been teaching me
naughty British swears. He's a delightfully entertaining
cuntybollocks, that one.*

MILES: *Shut up.*

OWEN: *Shut up.*

MILES: *You need to be upfront with Martin about this,
Owen. Sooner the better. I gotta go, Sir Brad Pitt's calling.*

DYLAN: *Shut up.*

OWEN: *Shut up.*

DYLAN: *Hey. Just wanted to say that Frankie is really
great. Like, really great. Sam obviously loves her, and
she's probably the coolest woman you've ever liked. And
when we had brunch I could tell you like her a lot. So I
hope it works out. Don't fuck it up.*

OWEN: *Did you just have therapy or something?*

DYLAN: *Yeah. I'm feeling very open right now. You
cuntpuddle.*

OWEN: *Love you, fuckwit.*

DYLAN: *Fuckety bye, boo.*

OWEN: *Hey. You look really cute sitting over there watching shark attacks with my son.*

FRANKIE: *Cute like Jerry Seinfeld, you mean?*

OWEN: *Cute like I want you to crawl across the floor and unzip me with your teeth.*

FRANKIE: *Maybe I'll wait until Sam's asleep.*

OWEN: *Up to you. Need to ask you something. I have to call Martin back. I feel like I should tell him about us. Thoughts?*

FRANKIE: *No. My first thought is NO. My next thought is FUCK NO. In conclusion: Please fuck no.*

OWEN: *So you don't want me to tell him about us screwing is what you're saying.*

FRANKIE: *First of all--why does he need to know that, and secondly I don't want him to know that. Third, the word "us" makes me nervous.*

OWEN: *Can't have "nervous" without "us."*

FRANKIE: *It's not you, it's me.*

OWEN: *Oh I know.*

FRANKIE: *<raised middle finger emoji>*

OWEN: *;) I won't tell Martin about how you're obsessed with my big, hard cock if you don't want me to.*

FRANKIE: *Fantastic. I won't tell Entertainment Weekly about your nefarious edging technique.*

OWEN: *You should definitely tell them about how you rode my face in the back of a limo though.*

FRANKIE: *Hold that thought while I go grab your son a milk from the minibar.*

OWEN: *I'll go into the bedroom to call Martin and not talk about how delicious your pussy is with him.*

FRANKIE: *Too far.*

OWEN: *;)*

26

OWEN

"Martin Hancock's office." Martin's assistant always answers the phone sounding like a bored asshole who thinks you're an asshole for calling him.

So I always try to sound like an asshole who thinks he's an asshole for making me talk to him. "Hey. Returning his call."

"Lemme see if I can get him."

"Great. Can't wait to find out."

"Fantastic. Please hold."

Asshole.

Now I have to pretend I understand Australian slang and sound like the guy who didn't have shower sex with my manager's favorite niece the other day in New York.

"G'day. How ya goin'? Just checkin' in."

"G'day! I'm good. Everything's good. Nothing to report, really. Everything's going well."

"Oh yeah? Had a squizz at your notes on the pilot script. They're really funny. I think the next draft is the *winnah*. They should be able to hire a writing staff and get things goin'."

What the fuck is a squizz? Sounds like what his niece did to me in the shower.

"Cool, yeah. Actually, Frankie helped out with those notes. The other day. At the airport."

"She did, eh?"

"Yeah, just…you know. We were talking. She gave me a few ideas for things. She's really, really funny. Really funny. I think she's a really funny comedian. She's good at stand-up, and she'd probably do really well on a writing staff. I was thinking maybe she could open for me one of these nights. I know you've booked all the opening guys already, but y'know. If someone gets sick last minute or something. She could be the pinch hitter."

"Uh-huh. She's working out for you, then? As Sam's nanny?"

"Yes. Definitely. She's working out for Sam, yes. She's great with him. He thinks she's great. I don't get to spend as much time with her, obviously, as Sam does. But she's great. And really funny."

"Aw, shit… Tyler—get off the line."

"Yes, sir." There's a click when the asshole assistant hangs up.

"Shit. Owen. Did you root my niece?"

"I don't… I'm not sure what *root* is, but I don't think I did."

"Yeah, you did." I can hear him scrubbing his tanned, stubbly face. "Shhhhit. Okay. I don't know why I didn't see that coming. I didn't think she was your type."

"I… I was just saying how funny she is."

"Okay. Listen. You didn't tell me anything. All right? I don't know anything."

"I *didn't* tell you anything."

"Do *not* tell anyone in the business that you've slept with her. Not even your brothers. You haven't told anyone, have you?"

"I didn't… I haven't…"

Shit.

"I have issues with nepotism, okay? I mean, it's just comedy, I know. It's Hollywood, not the White House. I know that, mate. But for you, even… This is your first solo tour and your first TV deal. You don't want to look like you're thinking with your dick. And if you're angling to give Frankie her first big break, it's *bettah* for her if it doesn't look like you gave it to her because she gave you a ripper gobby—ya know what I mean?"

"I don't know what a *ripper gobby* means, no. But that's not why I want to give her a break. I just think she's funny and talented."

"Yeah. She's funny. She'll get her big break one way or another. Look, I have clients who are attractive female comedians, and it's hard enough for them out there without having to deal with rumors that they got to where they are by bangin' their way to the middle."

"I know. I definitely don't want her to have to deal with that. I just wanted to make sure you're cool with—"

"I don't know anything."

"Got it."

He sighs. "Ask Frankie if she's got a writing sample. Do not send it to me. Do not tell her I know about the two of you. If she's interested in a writer's assistant job for your show, send it to Barry Weiner. Do it *soonah rathah* than *latah*. Do not tell him she's your kid's nanny, and definitely do not tell him you're havin' a naughty with her. Ya got that?"

"Understood."

"Right. You're my client and I will always protect your interests. But if you fuck things up for her, I will cut off your balls and shove them up Howie Mandel's asshole. Call me if you need anything."

He hangs up, leaving me with the actual worst image I've ever had in my head.

That did not go the way I thought it would.

But his advice is good. I think. I certainly never thought of any of those things he mentioned. Guess that's why he gets ten percent of me.

ME: *BTW don't tell anyone in the business about me and Frankie.*

DYLAN: *I only told my buddy Sir Patrick Stewart, and he won't tell anyone. He's a vault.*

ME: *Shut up, Dylan.*

MILES: *Shut up, Dylan. And I'm a fucking attorney. I actually am a vault.*

DYLAN: *Shut up, Miles. Actors can be vaults too. I still haven't told anyone about your third nipple.*

MILES: *I can actually sue you for slander, asshole.*

ME: *Thanks for not making this about me, assholes.*

MILES: *Poor little middle child.*

DYLAN: *Haven't told anyone about your tiny penis either, Owen.*

ME: *<raised middle finger emoji>*

I take a deep breath before opening the sliding door from the bedroom to the rest of the suite.

Sam's and Frankie's eyes are glued to the big screen, and I can tell from the music score that something's about to get attacked by a shark. Two seconds later, they both grimace and shout at the screen and then high-five each other. They're so fucking cute together I can just feel every single one of my sperm cells jockeying to impregnate that woman.

But that can't happen.

Not yet anyway.

"Hey, *Fawthah!*" Sam says when he sees me. He's

been obsessed with the Boston accent ever since we got here last night. "Whaddya doin' in *theyuh*? *Tawkin'* on the phone, or what?"

"My boy's wicked *smaht*."

Frankie gets up from the floor and messes up Sam's hair. "Hey, you want a *chawklit bah* or somethin' from the mini*bah*, kid?"

"Yeah! Sumthin' with nuts!"

"And *buttahscawtch*?"

"Yeaaaahhhh!"

I follow her over to the minibar. She smells good, and I want to stick my face in the crook of her neck and just inhale her for like half an hour or the rest of my life maybe. But she's going to take Sam out to the Museum of Science in a bit, and I have to do a couple of interviews and then the show. And I have to figure out how to help her without fucking anyone over or pissing anyone off.

She watches me while picking out a Snickers bar. "You okay? You look perplexed."

"Yeah. Just thinking about the sitcom."

"Trying to come up with more funny words for…" she lowers her voice, "schlongs?"

"Always. I just wish it was a cooler show. I mean, would *you* want to watch it?"

"Of course I'm going to watch it."

Fuck, I want to kiss her. I want to kiss her for, like, half an hour or the rest of my life, probably.

"Even if you weren't obsessed with my schlong, I mean."

I get an exaggerated eye-roll and a surreptitious elbow to the ribs for that. "Hey, there's nothing wrong with cheesy family sitcoms. Your show will make people happy. It will make them laugh because they'll get all the jokes. It will make them go awww and feel comfortable about life and keep them company when they're at home alone. It's entertainment. Don't overthink it."

Well, shit. She might want to work on my show after all.

"Says the heckler who criticized all of my tweets."

"Not all of them. And maybe that was entertainment for me."

"So do you have a writing sample?"

"What do you mean?"

"Like for a half-hour sitcom? Anything in script form."

"I wrote an episode of *The Suite Life of Zach and Cody* where Zach and Cody find out there's a big orgy going on in one of the hotel suites and they get laid. I was drunk when I wrote it. It's disgusting but also very sweet and funny."

"That is something I need to read immediately. Do you have the file with you?"

"Yeah, I brought my laptop. Why?"

"Can you email it to me? I just... I know you'll need a job again once we're back in LA. I can't promise anything, but if you're interested, I was thinking I could put you up for the writer's assistant gig."

I can't read the expression on her face at all because she's totally expressionless.

Then she gets all teary-eyed, looks down, and whispers, "I really wish I could kiss you right now."

"Me too."

"Thank you. I mean, I know it's a long shot, but I'd really appreciate that."

"Good. Well, send me that script, and we'll see. They aren't hiring just yet, but definitely before we get back to LA."

"Okay."

"Frankie!!! The *hammahhead shawks*! The *hammahhead shawks*!"

"Be right there!" She nudges my arm and affects a Boston accent again. "I gotta blast."

"Wicked *pissah*."

I want to do so many things to her that are disgusting but also very sweet and funny for half an hour or the rest of my life.

27

FRANKIE

I've never been to Detroit before. It's a lot nicer than I thought it would be. I guess I was expecting to get shot at by gangs or something.

Instead, I'm in the lobby of a fancy hotel, bantering with a woman called Grammie Todd. She's Nico Todd's grandmother. And Shane Miller's wife's grandmother. She also knows Dylan Brodie from when he played Shane Miller's brother on *That's So Wizard.* This old lady knows a lot of hot guys. I can't tell if she's in her sixties or seventies or eighties, but she's really spunky and sarcastic and probably the coolest grandma I've ever met. She scares the shit out of me, but I really want her to like me and I desperately want to be her when I grow up. If Garfield is Sam's spirit animal, then Grammie Todd is mine.

She's been comped for Owen's show tonight, and

she offered to sit with Sam in the audience and look after him for a while before the show so I can "have a little break." And I'm fifty percent sure that Grammie has no idea my break will involve boning Sam's dad in his hotel room, but I'm also fifty percent sure that Grammie knows everything about everyone. Which is why she scares the shit out of me. And why I adore her so much.

"I remember meeting this fellow on the *Wizard* set when Dylan was on the show," she tells me while grinning at Owen. "Owen hadn't grown into his face yet. So scrawny. All nose and chin and knees and elbows and fart jokes. Look how far he's come. All grown into his face and getting paid to tell fart jokes."

"Ain't life grand?" he says. "Hey, Sam. Whatever Grammie Todd tells you about me today, just remember—she's trying to get me back for the time I got her to sit on a whoopie cushion in front of about fifty people. I've actually been cool my whole life."

"You mean up until I met you, right?" Sam replies.

Grammie and I both lean forward to high-five that kid.

Owen's phone vibrates. When he checks it, he says he has to take the call, quickly gives Sam a hug, shakes Grammie's hand, and tells me he'll "see me later," then walks off.

There's a good chance his penis will be inside me

in around fifteen minutes, but I'm pretty sure it's not obvious that that's why I'm squeezing my thighs together. I'm positive Sam has no idea his dad and I spend time together when he's asleep or not around. He recently started reading Harry Potter, so he doesn't care much about anything else now.

When I glance over at Grammie, though, she has an elfish glint in her eye as she smirks at me.

"You know... You never look at each other at the same time, you and Owen. But when you do look at each other, your eyes light up. Both of you. If I had a heart, I'd find it rather adorable."

My stupid nose is tingling and I have to clear my stupid throat before responding. "Really? Well, if I had a heart, I'd find that rather endearing."

"So much easier being a heartless asshole." She winks at me.

"It's the only way to live."

"Why don't you say goodbye to Sam now and I'll take him to the restaurant for an early dinner. Off you go."

I explain the cheese thing to her, tell Sam I'll see him later, and then head up to Owen's penis—I mean his hotel room.

I don't even go to my room to freshen up first because I'm already freshened.

Owen opens the door two seconds after I've knocked on it, and he looks exactly as anxious as I feel in my lady parts.

He takes my arm and pulls me inside. "Hi. Did you bring your ukulele?"

"Um. It's in my suitcase. I don't usually do sex stuff with my uke, but what did you have in mind?"

"I love that you're open to trying new sex stuff with me, and I definitely want to circle back to this topic. But I meant for your stand-up. As my opening act tonight."

"What?"

"Martin just told me the local comedian who was supposed to open for me tonight has food poisoning. He had to cancel. I don't want Martin to find a replacement because I have someone."

I still don't understand. "Who?"

"You, dummy."

"Wait. What?"

"Let me put it to you this way: I've got good news and bad news. The bad news is you and I aren't going to have sex right now. The good news is it's because you have to get ready to open for me at the theater tonight. More bad news is it'll be in front of a sold-out crowd of about seventeen hundred people."

I shove his stupid beautiful bicep. "Shut. Up."

"We both know I'll never do that."

"Okay, but seriously. What?! Tonight?"

"Yeah, in, like, two and a half hours."

"Holy shit! Are you sure?"

He laughs, shaking his head. "Course I'm sure. Detroit and I will be lucky to have you."

What is this feeling in my chest?

What are these words that are stuck in my throat?

I have never told any man other than my father that I love him before. And maybe my uncle when he bought me and my friends beer that time when I was seventeen. But never any man I'm not related to. Unless you count those pictures of Owen Brodie that I had up on my wall when I was a teenager. So I guess it makes sense that I have this terrible urge to tell the real Owen Brodie that I love him right now. But it also doesn't make any sense at all because how can I love Owen Brodie?

He's being so nice to me lately, I don't even know who he is or who we are anymore, so I don't know how to be with him.

I guess he can see that in my expression, so he says, "Would it be easier for you to get into comedy mode if I'm a dick to you?"

"Yes. Except that even asking me that is so perfect that if you're a dick to me, it would be very un-dickish."

"What a conundrum."

I start pacing around. "So I need to do fifteen minutes of material, right?"

"Yeah. Just do your mom stuff and a break-up song. Maybe a Bill Murray impression or two."

"Shit. I didn't bring any stand-up outfits."

"Just wear what you're wearing. Don't shave your face. You can borrow my glasses so you'll look more likable." He grins. "Who cares what you're wearing. You'll be terrible no matter what. Better?"

"Better."

"Good. You want to run your act by me, or do you want to be alone?"

"Alone. But thank you. But that was very nice of you to offer, so screw you."

"I was going to heckle you, but go on. Get out of here, and I hope you bomb, you asshole."

"I'm going to kill so hard, you'll look like an amateur."

"Well, I won't *look* like an amateur, but I might sound like one."

I grab his stupid professionally handsome face and kiss him so hard. "Thank you. Did I say thank you? Thank you. I can't even—I can't believe—I don't know how to…"

"Just do your thing and have fun." He pats me on the butt as I open the door. "You're wearing fancy lingerie under those clothes, aren't you?"

I smirk at him over my shoulder. "Now you'll never know."

"Dammit." He steps in front of me to stand in front of the door. "I mean, we still have time for a quickie."

"If you don't get out of my way, I will cut you."

"Fair enough." He opens the door for me. "Break a leg."

"Thanks again." I kiss him again. And then again because his face is so stupidly handsome and smirky and he's being so damn sweet.

"Get outta here. But break a leg. And I'll think up some creative ways to use that ukulele for sex stuff next time we get a babysitter."

OWEN

I have never been so nervous for another person in my life.

That's not true.

I was exactly this nervous when Sam had to recite three lines as a turkey in his school play last year. But he did fine. So will Frankie. Better than fine, I'm sure of it.

I didn't tell her, but I just started following her on Twitter finally. People won't think I'm banging her just because I'm following her on there. It's not like I'm boning Amy Schumer or Ricky Gervais—not that they follow me back. *Assholes.*

She takes the stage, holding her ukulele. I stand offstage, in the wings, watching her. I can see Sam and Grammie in the front row. Grammie has my video camera. She agreed to film Frankie's act. That was really great of her, but I should have asked

Martin to make sure Grammie Todd sits somewhere I can't see her because I'll probably spend my entire act stressing out because the woman never laughs. She's worse than a heckler because she just quietly judges me while smirking. Ever since I was a kid. But I kind of love her anyway, and I really love that Frankie loves her.

And I love that the local comedian got food poisoning so Frankie can replace him.

I love that I could give her this opportunity.

I love that Sam gets to watch her do her thing on a big stage, in front of a big audience.

I just love everything about this.

And *her*.

She places her uke on top of the stool and picks up the microphone. "Hello, Detroit? Am I in the right place? This is Detroit, right?"

She gets a lot of cheers and claps for that.

"I'm so happy to be here. I actually have an ex-boyfriend from Detroit." She peers out into the audience. "You here, Justin?"

Several dudes who may or may not be named Justin call out, "Yeah, baby!"

"Right, well, I don't know if you know this about me—strangers who have no idea who I am and those guys who just said *Yeah, baby!*—but I have nine ex-boyfriends named Justin. Justin Number Six was the best...to mess around with after he broke up with me. This was in LA, where I live. He was an actor who had bit parts in, like, seventy thousand terrible shows and movies, but he was a fun guy—just ask him—and he was friends with a lot of famous people. So when we were dating we'd be at a coffee shop or whatever, talking about him and all seventy thousand of the terrible shows and movies he was in and how he's obsessed with one day being in a Marvel movie, and his cell phone would ring. He'd always get this look on his face when he looked at the Caller ID, and then he'd hold his finger up to me and say, 'I gotta take this, babe. It's Liam Hemsworth. We've been playing phone tag. It's a whole thing.' Or 'I gotta take this. It's Jennifer Love Hewitt. She wants to know about a cleanse I just did.' But it was always these—forgive me—B-list celebrities.

"So after we broke up, I'd call him from restaurant phones or a couple of burner phones I bought just for this, and I'd leave voice messages and be like… 'G'day, Justin. This is Chris Hemsworth. The *bettah* Hemsworth. Stop wasting your time slummin' with my *brothah,* mate. I had my guys write a *paht* for you in my next movie, *Thor: Clash of the Thunder-fahts.* Call the chairman of Disney to let him know you want the job. He's expecting your call. The name of the guy you'll play is *Nevah Gonnabee.* So just give the chairman of Disney a ring and tell him you're the guy Chris Hemsworth said is *Nevah Gonnabee* in the next Thor movie."

She has to pause for the laughter to subside before continuing.

"And then right after that message I left this one: 'Hello, Justin? This is Taika Waititi, *directah* of the next Thor movie which has just been given the new title of *Thor: Blast of the Air Biscuit*. I just heard what Chris told you, and I'm afraid he got it wrong. You need to call *me* back to let me know that you want the *paht* we had written for you. The name of the *charactah* you'd play is Idiot Loserdick. So find my private *numbah*, call me back, tell me you're the Idiot Loserdick who thinks he should be in a *Mahvel* movie, and we'll set you up.'"

She gets a lot of applause and laughs for that.

She really is killing, and she looks so comfortable out there.

"Yeah, I mostly left messages from celebrities with Aussie or Kiwi accents because my mum's from Australia…"

She does her bit about emails her mom's sent her with joke ideas, which is so cute. Then she segues with: "Speaking of songs my mum used to listen to that don't sound *too much* like the one I'm about to sing…here's a little something I wrote about Justin Number Six after getting a booty text from him a couple of months following our breakup."

She puts the mic back on the stand, picks up her ukulele, strums it a few times, then starts singing like Carly Simon.

Sort of.

"You showed up on my cell phone
Like you fully expected to bone
Even though it was just two months ago
You dumped me to date Emma Stone

You're such a cocky arrogant conceited asshole douche
Who will never be in a Marvel movie
Or series
And you will also never be in me again
Never be in me again

But
I can't complain
At least I got a funny bit out of it
You're such a cocky arrogant conceited asshole douche
At least I got a half-decent song out of it
Didn't I?
Did I?
I did

I had some drinks– they were very alcoholic
So alcoholic
And
You can kiss my ass
But not really because I won't let you near it
Kiss my ass
You probably really want to, don't you?

But I won't let you
Let you
Won't let you."

Five minutes later, she's basically brought the house down.

If I weren't so happy for her, I really would be pissed at her for making me look bad.

Or sound bad.

And worried about what kind of song she'd write about me for her act if things end between us.

Not that I want things to end for us.

Not that they've officially started.

But I don't even have time to think about any of that because she walks off stage and straight into my arms.

She's glowing.

"That was such a rush!" she says.

"You totally killed."

"I know! Who even am I?"

"You're a superstar."

"I think I might be!"

"I know you are. I'm so happy for you."

"Oh my God, I love you!"

Is what I think I hear her say just as I realize someone could see us hugging like this, pull away from her, and tell her, "We can't let anyone see us together—I'll meet you in my dressing room after. Wait—what?"

"Nothing. Shut up! Go!"

She looks horrified.

Like her life is over.

And then she turns and walks away from me, toward backstage.

I have to do around seventy minutes of material, make people laugh, and *not* wonder if I just fucked up a really important moment with the most important woman in my life right now.

Lady Hilarious McFunnyPants, ladies and gentlemen.

Always finding fresh new ways to ruin my act.

On with the show.

FRANKIE

"How many fart jokes did you tell? Did you use the ninja one?" my dad asks.

"No! None! Sam was in the audience, so I didn't want to take any chances."

I'm in the empty theater lobby, talking to my parents on the phone. There was loud applause inside the theater a few minutes ago, which means Owen is doing his encore now. My parents are so excited to hear that I just performed in front of a big audience that I've almost forgotten the tiny incident from a little over an hour ago. The one where, for the first time in my life, I said "I love you" to a man I'm not related to and he responded by telling me we need to make sure no one sees us together.

That little incident.

I had *almost* forgotten about it.

And almost worn out the soles of my shoes and

the carpet from pacing back and forth around this lobby for fifty minutes. I was too scared to walk around outside. But being able to hear Owen's voice through the walls was torture.

Seeing the notification that @theowenbrodie started following me on Twitter almost made things a little less terrible.

Almost.

"Fancy Frankie, we're gonna start calling you," my mum says. "Oh, just wait 'til I tell everyone at the salon. They're gonna shit bricks. Did you talk about me and my jokes?"

"Of course I did. Detroit loved you."

"Strewth, I bet they did! Oh, I can't wait to see it on YouTube. I'll post it on my Facebook!"

"Me too. Heck, I'll even start a TikTok and post the YouTube on there!"

"That's not how TikTok works, Daddy."

"Well, I tried."

I can hear loud applause again, and the doors from the inside theater to the lobby open up.

"I have to go now, you guys."

I have to figure out how to hide from Owen Brodie for the rest of the tour while still fulfilling my nanny duties.

"We're so proud of you, baby girl. Let us know as soon as the YouTube's up!"

"I will."

"Break a leg, darlin'."

"Already did, Daddy. You say that *before* a show—but thank you. Love you, bye!"

I hang up and spot Grammie and Sam among the crowd of people pouring into the lobby.

Sam looks tired but happy. Grammie looks exactly like she looked the whole time we were talking at the hotel—mischievous and like she might say something that will break you in half at any moment.

"How was it? Did you have fun?"

"You were awesome! I liked it when you talked in those accents and sang that song."

"Thanks, man."

Grammie holds the video camera out to me. "I got your entire act on tape. You were magnificent."

I can't tell if she's being sarcastic or not.

"I'm not being sarcastic," she explains, continuing to smirk and deadpan. "I don't know how to make my face or my voice do anything other than this."

"Well, thank you so much for recording it."

"Did you not watch Owen's part?" Now Grammie is studying my face, so I look away.

Sam yawns. "Are we going back to the hotel now? I have to go to bed."

Every other seven-year-old on Earth needs to be put to bed twelve times in a row, but this kid actually requests bedtime.

"We just have the one car here. I can text your dad to ask him to hurry up."

When I look at my phone, I find a message from Owen.

OWEN: *Where are you? Why aren't you in my dressing room?*
ME: *In the lobby with Sam and Grammie. Sam wants to go to bed.*
OWEN: *Tell them I need to talk to you back here. Ask them to wait for us in the lobby.*
ME: *No thanks!*
OWEN: *Frankie. Get your ass back here right now. We need to talk.*
ME: *We really don't.*
OWEN: *Don't make me come out there and get you.*
ME: *Oh my God. Fine.*

I ask Grammie and Sam to give us fifteen minutes and then head backstage. On my way, a few people pat me on the back and tell me I was hilarious, which feels pretty great. It almost makes me forget how much I dread seeing and talking to Owen about the tiny moment from just over an hour ago.

Almost.

I knock on the door to his dressing room. When he opens it, he looks so handsome I want to slap him and so stressed out I want to make him a cup of chamomile tea. And then slap him. He's taken his glasses off, so he's fair game.

He steps aside, ushering me in, and then locks the

door behind me. I'm expecting some kind of lecture, like *You can't love me.* Or *This is show* business *not show* nannies with benefits.

Instead he paces around, combing his fingers through his hair. So I just stand near the door, arms crossed. It's a nice dressing room. Kind of fancy, even. Very clean. I know this because I am staring at every single thing in this room that isn't Owen Brodie.

"Frankie."

"Thanks for following me on Twitter," I say to his feet. "I already got a bunch of new followers."

"That's great. But that's not what I want to talk about, and you know it."

"Well, what you want to talk about is what I *don't* want to talk about, and you know it."

"Listen to me." He backs me up against a wall and holds my chin up so I have to look at him. "When I talked to Martin back in Boston, he figured out that we're…having intimate relations. I didn't tell him because you didn't want me to. But he figured it out, and he didn't want me to tell *you* that he knows. I told him I want you to open for me if the opportunity comes up. I told him I want to help you get a job in the business when the tour is over. He gave me some very compelling reasons why people shouldn't know we're…having intimate relations. That's why I said we shouldn't let people see us like that. For your sake. For your career. You get that?"

"Yeah. Fine. I get it."

"I love you too, Frankie."

I try to wriggle away from him. "You don't have to say that just because I said it."

He holds on to my arms, pinning me against the damn wall. "No fucking kidding. I'm saying it because I want to say it. Because it's how I feel."

"Well that's fucking adorable, but we don't have to say it ever again."

"Too fucking bad if you don't want to hear it because I'm going to keep saying it. I love you, Frankie." He grabs my face. "You're a little shit and you're driving me insane, but I can't believe how much I love you." He dips down to kiss me.

I've never been kissed like this before. So hard and soft at the same time. He's giving me life and taking my breath away, and he's the only person who has ever been able to do this. He could literally devour all of me with his mouth right now, slowly or all at once, and I would be fine with that.

When he finally takes a moment to breathe, I whisper, "I love you." I'm light-headed and my heart is racing, but I feel so good all of a sudden, it's all I can say. "I love you."

In my mind, there's no one outside this room, no one waiting for us in the lobby at this moment. There's just us and a couple of buttons that need to be unbuttoned, two zippers that need to be unzipped, and two pairs of pants and undies that will be hastily pulled down. We had the "I'm on the pill/I'm clean" convo back in Ohio, so he just needs to put it in me.

"Tell me again," I manage to say as I remove everything that's covering me from the waist down so I can hop up and wrap my legs around him.

"I love you." He groans, pressing himself inside me.

I've never been fucked like this before. So hard and soft at the same time. Fast but purposeful. Not a rush to get to the finish line, just a rush to get to each other. The best kind of rush I've ever felt. Better than making people laugh. It's not the setup and it's not the punchline. It's not funny and it's not even scary.

It's just Owen Brodie and me and the thing we've probably been trying to say to each other all along.

"I love you."

Owen Brodie @theowenbrodie
Thanks for the laughs, Detroit. And thanks to
@frankiesayrelax for opening for me.
#GladImNotAJustin

Frankie Hogan @frankiesayrelax
Replying to @theowenbrodie
Thanks for letting me be funnier than you in Detroit!
#YouCantHandleBeingAJustin

Owen Brodie @theowenbrodie
Replying to @frankiesayrelax
#IBetYouThinkThisTweetIsAboutYou

Frankie Hogan @frankiesayrelax
Replying to @theowenbrodie
#IBetYouThinkAllTweetsAreAboutYou

Owen Brodie @theowenbrodie
Replying to @frankiesayrelax
#NopeJustYours

Frankie Hogan @frankiesayrelax
Replying to @theowenbrodie
#PleaseGetOverYourself

Owen Brodie @theowenbrodie
Replying to @frankiesayrelax
;)

Frankie Hogan @frankiesayrelax
Replying to @theowenbrodie
<face with rolling eyes emoji>

FRANKIE

Texas is big, hot, and full of calories.

Owen did his show in Houston last night, and I stayed with Sam at the hotel so his parents could enjoy being in the audience. We're all spending the day at the Brodie residence in this small town about a half hour from the city. By "spending the day" here, I mean eating and drinking everything Bonnie Lyn Brodie brings out from the kitchen and anything Owen's father grills out here on the patio. So far, this has included barbecue chicken and ribs (they apologized for not having a third meat), cornbread, taco salad with extra cheese, ice cream, chicken-fried steak, deep-fried okra, and mashed potatoes covered in gravy. There has been no discernible break between lunch and early supper, aside from a change of plates and cutlery. Everything is delicious, and I can't *not* eat all of it. I also can't keep the button fastened on my jeans anymore. Or breathe. Or remember what day it is. Because of the bottomless pitcher of Texas Tea for the grown-ups.

I don't even want to know what's in Texas Tea, but I'm pretty sure there's no tea in it. It's about six different types of liquor, Coke, a bunch of ice, and a lemon garnish. I am definitely making this when I get back to LA.

Sam can no longer sit up, so he's been lying down beside me on the long bench at the family-size table. This has not stopped him from consuming food or drinking his fifth Dr. Pepper from a long, curly straw. It's hard not to feel at home in a place where you're this well-fed.

Mama Brodie has been so busy serving us that I haven't actually seen her eat or drink anything, but I'd say she's about one and a half sheets to the wind while still looking like Grace Kelly. She's been telling a story about adolescent Owen for the past twenty minutes but keeps getting sidetracked and forgetting details and asking her husband to remind her of the names of people. "Ohhhh and get this, y'all! Owen!"

"Yes, Mama."

"Remember the time we ran into that actor at that restaurant? What was his name? The old fella from *Back to the Future*?"

"Christopher Lloyd," Owen says.

"Christopher Lloyd! He was there eating by himself in that fancy restaurant, and you went over to him and asked for his autograph, and he was so mean to you."

"That wasn't Christopher Lloyd," Joe tells her. "That was Mandy Patinkin from *The Princess Bride*, and it was at a deli, and he wasn't mean to him."

"Oh, I love that movie! Remember the first time you watched that movie, Owen? Frankie, he was so cute. He went around saying, 'As you wish' for months afterward."

Joe calmly shakes his head. "That was Dylan. Owen kept saying, 'My name is Inigo Montoya. You killed my father. Prepare to die.'"

Mr. Brodie's Inigo Montoya impression is flawless, and he is so handsome it's just embarrassing to look at him. It feels like my eyeballs have been blushing ever since we got here. I've seen Miles Brodie in pictures around this house now, as well as his young daughter Macy, and can safely say that the entire Brodie family is so attractive it actually makes it seem normal for them to be that ridiculously good-looking. Like, it's the rest of us who are genetically weird for not having jawlines that you could saw timber with.

"Pops" Brodie was a soap star in LA for about twenty-five years, and then he and Mrs. Brodie moved here, to a suburb of Houston, to flip houses and sip cocktails.

I mean, I love my parents a lot, but I would very much like for these people to adopt me.

Mama Brodie is now off on a tangent about how they definitely saw Christopher Lloyd from *Back to the Future* somewhere and one of the brothers asked for his autograph and he was mean.

Before we'd left the hotel, Owen reminded me that we still need to pretend we aren't "being intimate" with each other while we're around Sam or his parents, since his dad still counts as being "in the business" because he's in touch with his Hollywood friends. I'm fine with that because it turns out being discrete is half the fun.

We had the car service drive us out here. Owen and I are supposed to take a cab back to the hotel while Sam stays the night with his grandparents. We've been looking forward to a "nookie night" for ages, it seems. Although I guess technically we haven't actually known each other for ages. It only feels that way.

Owen winks at me from across the table when his parents are busy arguing with each other about older male celebrities from 80s movies. *How's Sam doing down there?* he mouths to me.

I give him the thumbs-up.

"You finished with that Dr. Pepper, Sammy?"

He belches and grins when mumbling, "Don't call me Sammy."

It's our new thing. "Oh, I thought you liked it when I call you Sammy."

"I do not."

"Hey, doodlebug!" Bonnie Lyn ducks down so she can see him under the table. "I sure do hope you saved room for chocolate pecan pie, little man. Alla y'all!" She claps her hands together. "Are we ready for dessert? Yay or nay?"

There's a chorus of nays, even from Sam.

"Lemme help you clean up, Mama. I should get Frankie back to the hotel so she can take a nap."

"Aw, come on now. Don't go yet. I'll make a fresh pot of coffee."

"We really need to get going. She gets cranky if she doesn't get her after-supper nap."

I roll my eyes at him. Hopefully the other Brodies don't share Owen's belief that my eye-roll means I want to have intimate relations with him. I mean, I do want that, but that's not what the eye-roll means.

"Frank?" Sam's been calling me Frank since lunchtime because he's too full and lazy to add the "ie" at the end. "Why can't you and my dad stay here too? This house is so big."

"Oh, well, we still have the hotel rooms reserved, so…"

"But I counted five bedrooms. And did you see how big the shower is in the upstairs bathroom? You and Dad could both fit in there like in Atlanta."

Spit-take.

"Whaaat? We didn't—That never—"

"We don't—That's not what…" Owen's trying

really hard to straighten Sam out, but he can't keep a straight face and also Sam's right.

We did have a very quiet quickie shower together in the middle of the night in Atlanta when it seemed like Sam was fast asleep.

"Oh, we're real big on couples shower time around here, hons. Good for the planet." Bonnie Lyn gives me a long, slow wink just like her son did.

"Not a couple! Lemme help you clear the table." I attempt to stand up, but the earth starts spinning and the zipper on my jeans opens up. They're too tight to fall off and also so tight that I will probably have to ask one of these good people to cut me out of them in around half an hour so I can pee. "Schmeckler," I mutter.

"I got this," Owen states, but then he tries to stand up and also plops right back down on the bench. "Fuddrucker," he mumbles.

"Y'all had best plan on staying the night here," Joe tells us as he stands up to help his wife clear the table. "There's plenty of room, in and out of the showers."

"We aren't..." Owen is too full and sleepy to complete the sentence with anything other than a groan.

"We didn't..." I can't even remember what it is we're trying to convince people of anymore.

"It's fine, sugars. Dylan told us not to talk about it with anyone 'in the business.'"

"It was Miles who told us that," Joe corrects her. "But yeah."

Mama Brodie sticks her tongue out at her husband as they carry plates to the kitchen.

"Are you my dad's girlfriend now?" Sam asks. He isn't even looking at me. He's just staring at the Dr. Pepper can that's resting on his chest.

"Your dad and I have become friends," I explain to him. "He was just helping me with something in the bathroom that time."

"More like *you* were helping *me* with something," Owen snickers.

I give him a look—*Dude. Seriously?*

"Welp. I guess nobody's helping anyone with anything tonight, then," I say to Owen. I'm not even sad about it.

"Don't be so sure," he says. His forehead is attached to the top of the table.

"I think you guys are funny together," Sam whispers, barely loud enough for me to hear. And then he falls asleep and the Dr. Pepper can falls to the floor.

I just watch that can roll away, thinking how nice it must be to be able to move.

Sam's not wrong. Owen and I *are* funny together. I have no idea if we'll be funny together once we get back to LA, but I'm having the funniest summer of my life.

I don't think I want it to end.

271

32

OWEN: *You still awake?*

FRANKIE: *Eyes are open. Brain doesn't work.*

OWEN: *Same. Feet don't work either. Was going to sneak into your room for quiet nookie. Tried crawling. But it was too hard.*

FRANKIE: *That's what she said.*

FRANKIE: *Wait. That wasn't funny. Never mind.*

OWEN: *Should we sext?*

FRANKIE: *I mean it's super sexy that you asked, so obviously I'm really turned on right now.*

OWEN: *Asshole.*

FRANKIE: *Is that supposed to be a sext? Because no butt stuff.*

OWEN: *You need a spanking. That's what I would do to your butt.*

OWEN: *Wait. That didn't sound sexy. Did it?*

FRANKIE: *No. Would you like me to talk about how big and hard your ding dong is?*

OWEN: *Yes.*

FRANKIE: *It's really big. So hard. I want to do stuff to it with my hands and my mouth and my vulcanite.*

FRANKIE: *Why the duck did it autocorrect to that? WHAT THE FUCK IS A VULCANITE?! I have never used that word in my life before.*

OWEN: *Stay focused, baby. Talk about my cocktail.*

OWEN: *Cock.*

OWEN: *<rooster emoji>*

OWEN: *<hot dog emoji>*

OWEN: *<bone emoji>*

OWEN: *<avocado emoji>*

OWEN: *Wait that was supposed to be <eggplant emoji>*

FRANKIE: *No more food. No more.*

FRANKIE: *I looked up vulcanite. It's hard, black, vulcanized rubber. Which actually sounds filthier than vulva, so good job, phone.*

OWEN: *What are you going to do with your vulcanite?*

FRANKIE: *Made note so I can use that in a bit. Dibs.*

OWEN: *Focus!*

FRANKIE: *There is a large framed photo of the entire Brodie family staring at me in here and I'm wearing your mother's nightgown. It feels all kinds of wrong to write sexy stuff.*

OWEN: *Then take my mama's nightgown off and flip over.*

FRANKIE: *If I could move enough to get naked and flip*

over we'd be back at the hotel right now and you'd be flipping me over.

OWEN: *Oooh. That works.*

FRANKIE: *You aren't actually touching your Texas Longhorn right now are you?*

OWEN: *Yeah that's good.*

FRANKIE: *Owen.*

OWEN: *Oh yeah. So good.*

OWEN: *I'm just kidding. Should we just go to sleep?*

FRANKIE: *Is that lame? Are we old and boring already?*

OWEN: *You were already old and boring before I met you.*

FRANKIE: *Thank you.*

OWEN: *I love having you here with my family, Frankie. I hope it was fun for you.*

FRANKIE: *I love your family.*

OWEN: *They love you too.*

OWEN: *I love you.*

OWEN: *Did you fall asleep?*

OWEN: *You're asleep.*

OWEN: *Good night, beautiful.*

FRANKIE: *I'm awake again. I love you too.*

FRANKIE: *Did you go to sleep?*

FRANKIE: *Good night, Head Shot.*

33

MAMA BRODIE: *Owen Joseph Brodie. If you don't marry that girl, I will divorce your father and marry her myself. You hear me? I don't have much hope for Miles to remarry or for Dylan to marry at all, to be perfectly honest. But you actually have a chance at real happiness here. For yourself and the doodlebug. I feel very strongly about this. Tell him, Joe!*

MILES: *Wow. That's cold.*

DYLAN: *Interesting. That is exactly the opposite of what you usually tell me, Mama.*

MAMA BRODIE: *Shit on a biscuit. Wrong group. I hate this phone.*

POPS BRODIE: *Which part was it you wanted me to back you up on, darlin'? The bit about Miles and Dylan being a lost cause or the one about you divorcing me so you can marry your son's secret girlfriend that we aren't supposed to talk about?*

MAMA BRODIE: *I just love all you boys so much. Don't mind me.*

OWEN: *We're at the airport now, everyone. Great seeing you, Mama and Pops. Please don't talk about Frankie to anyone in the business and also please don't marry her. Obviously Miles and Dylan won't because they're pathetic.*

MILES: *<raised middle finger emoji>*

DYLAN: *<two raised middle finger emojis>*

OWEN

Everything in Vegas is all-you-can-eat, including the comedy shows.

I just finished my second performance of the day after three encores, and I am so ready to get back to the hotel. I've barely had time to see Sam and Frankie at all since we got here because I had to do so much promotional crap and we couldn't convince Sam to leave the air-conditioned hotel room to meet up with me for lunch. The thirty-second walk from the car to the hotel lobby was basically the worst half minute of his life, and he might never forgive me for it. And then he and Frankie complained to each other about desert heat, bright lights, and noisy crowds for half an hour straight. I hate to admit it, but they're a much cuter couple than Frankie and I are. Or Sam and me.

Frankie just goes with everything now, it seems —except desert heat, bright lights, and noisy crowds.

We're coming to the end of the tour, and all three of us are getting a little anxious. Frankie needs to figure out how she's going to pay the bills next month. Sam's ready to go home, but he keeps asking if Frankie's going to live with me in LA. Strangely enough, I would have no problem asking her to move in with me at this point, but not as a nanny. I just want to be able to shower with her every morning and come home to her every night. But I also want her to work on my series, and I haven't found out if I can hire her yet.

The only other time in my life where I felt stuck like this was when I was trying to make things work with Ashley for Sam's sake. Not that this feels the same in any other way. When I was with Ashley for the last couple of years of our marriage, I was miserable. I'm anything but miserable now. I just hate that I can't make a real move one way or another yet.

I'm about to call Frankie to let her know I'm heading back to the hotel soon, but I get a call from Martin's cell phone. He's probably on his way from his office to SoHo House or a movie screening right about now.

"Martin?"

"'Ey! How'd the shows go?"

"Really well. If the walls of this dressing room could talk, I'm pretty sure they'd talk really fast and make no sense because I swear there's a light dusting of cocaine on every surface in here."

"God, I love Vegas. So I've got good news. Your shows in San Francisco and LA are now sold out. You're finishing the tour just as strong as you started it."

"That's great. Are the opening acts confirmed?"

"Yeah, I don't foresee any of them getting food poisoning, but you never know."

"Fingers crossed."

"I talked to Barry Weiner and the showrunner a couple of hours ago. They got the greenlight to start hiring a writing staff, and they thought Frankie's sample was bonzer."

"And that's good?"

"Yeah, they loved it. I didn't mention that she's my niece, and they don't seem to know that she's your nanny, and I don't know if she's anything else to you."

"Right."

"Right. So you'll get a call from Barry soon, I'd imagine, to tell you that you can offer her the writer's assistant job."

"That's amazing. She'll be so stoked. She's got tons of followers on Twitter now, and she's lined up a couple of stand-up gigs next month in LA, but she was just looking at jobs online the other day and it was really disheartening."

"Yeah. You're talking about her like she's your missus, which is not something I need to hear."

"Right."

"Right. So here's the thing. You need to decide how to approach this with Frankie if you want to offer her the job."

Shit.

"I do. I have to offer her the job. I mean, she's already helped with the script so much. It'd be really shitty if I didn't."

"I do not disagree. You want my advice?"

I blow out a shaky breath. "Of course I do."

"You need to choose. If you're having relations with her—and I don't want to know if you are—you can stay with her and go ahead and be out in the open as a couple. But don't offer her a job unless you wanna hire her as a babysitter or full-time nanny when you're back in LA. Let her find her own way in the business. She already got a boost from opening for you."

"Uh-huh. Or?"

"Or offer her the job on your show and end things with her now. If you are indeed all up in her pink bits, that is. Try not to crack a fat if you're ever in the writers' room or on set with her. Pray to the gods of comedy that she doesn't sing a song about you in her act one day."

I don't think I realized exactly how much I love Frankie until this moment because I don't even care if she sings a funny song about how shitty I am in her stand-up act one day. If it makes her feel better and gets her the laughs, then great. If I break up with her, I'm no better than any of the Justins. Except in bed, obviously.

"How long do I have to decide?"

"Before offering her the job? You should really do it as soon as you can, mate. They're already getting submissions from agents, so she needs to sign a contract before they find someone else they like more than her. Or before Barry finds a hot, young writer he wants to bang."

"Why does Barry Weiner get to hire people he wants to bang and I don't?" I'm half joking, but only half. "I'm the fucking star of the show."

"Well, the difference is Barry hires them because he wants to bang them, but he never actually gets to bang them."

"So this business sucks for everyone is what you're saying."

"I mean, it's great for the women who don't end up banging Barry Weiner."

I can't even pretend to laugh at that.

"Listen, I'm not gonna tell you what to do, and I do not envy the position you're in. I want the best for both of you, I really do. I just don't know if the best thing for either of you is the same thing on a personal and professional level. Not right now anyway."

"Yeah. Okay. Lemme think about it. I'll let you know."

"Yeah, of course."

"Thanks, Marty. Fair dinkum."

"That's not the right way to use *fair dinkum*, and don't call me *Mahty*."

"Fair dinkum."

I hang up on him.

It's not fair dinkum. I'm still not sure what that phrase means, but it's not fair, and everyone in this business is a dinkum if they think I want to hire Frankie as a writer just because I'm having sex with her. Maybe if I tell the world I'm in love with her, things would be different.

Or maybe it would ruin everything.

I send her a text to ask if Sam's asleep.

FRANKIE: *He fell asleep on the floor while we were in the middle of playing Go Fish. Which is good because he was winning as usual. How was the show? You coming home?*

God. All I want is for her to be able to succeed in her career *and* to get a text from her asking if I'm coming home any time I'm not with her.

ME: *Yeah, babe. Show was great. I just have to call my brother, and then I'll have the driver pick me up.*

FRANKIE: *Good. I missed you today. Is that creepy to say? It feels creepy to write it. But I did. But get over it.*
ME: *I missed you too, creep. See you soon.*

For about thirty seconds, I think about calling Dylan because I know for a fact that he'll just tell me to hire Frankie, ask her to move in with me, and tell everyone else to fuck off. But he's a romantic at best and possibly a love addict at worst. And he doesn't have a kid, so he doesn't know what it's like to have to consider a little person's feelings and future with every decision he makes.

So I call the other brother. The one with the ex-wife and the little person and an even more pathetic love life than I've had in the past. He answers on the second ring.

"Hey."

"You on the other line with someone incredibly important?"

Miles exhales, long and loud. "I could tell you I just signed a multi-platinum Grammy-winning artist today, but it doesn't really matter because right now I'm trying to memorize the lyrics to 'Anything You Can Do' from *Annie Get Your Gun.*"

"Lemme guess. Father-daughter talent show?"

"What's sad is I really can sing better than Macy. But she wants it so badly."

"You're going to try to sing worse than her so she sounds better."

"I don't even know if it's possible. But I'll try."

"You at home right now?"

"Yeah. She's with her mom. Where are you?"

"Vegas, baby."

"You sound delighted to be there. What's up?,"

I exhale, long and loud, just like he did, and then I tell him what's up.

"Shit," is all he says when I'm done telling him.

"Yeah. I don't know what to do."

"Yeah you do. You just don't want anyone to get hurt because you're a good guy."

"So you think Martin's right? Those are my only viable options?"

He takes a very lawyerly moment to consider things before answering. "Who's to say? He knows what he's talking about. But this business can be tough for women no matter what. Maybe Frankie won't care what people think if she works on your show and people know you're a couple. Right?"

"Maybe. But what if she takes the job, everyone knows we're dating, it affects people's opinions of her, and then we break up? I just keep thinking about how I fucked things up with Ashley. It's hard to imagine things working out with Frankie in the long run. No matter how much I want them to."

"Hey. I haven't seen you with Frankie, but I can tell you're different with her than you were with Ashley. Apples and oranges. If we don't go into future relationships believing they'll be better than the ones we had with our exes, then what the fuck is the point? I mean, I don't know what the fuck the point is for me. Mama was probably right about that. But *you* can't think like that."

"Aw, come on. You've got as much of a shot at happiness as I do," I assure him. "You may be uglier and a bigger asshole than I am, but you *are* a lawyer. Chicks dig that. Never forget it."

"Thanks, man."

"Anytime… I mean, what if *you* find Frankie a job…?"

"Yeah, just let the lawyer fix all your problems."

"I mean, it's not like you're her uncle or her boyfriend."

"I have the same last name as you, idiot. Nut up, and make a choice. What's best for Sam?"

"He just wants her around. We all just want her around. But he doesn't understand how important it is for her to have a job and a career. I mean, if she works on the show, at least there's a chance we can be friends. Hopefully she'll still want to hang out with us sometimes. Come over for a cheese platter and Harry Potter marathon. I'll be able to see her in the writers' room occasionally."

"Kids are resilient. Except when it comes to digesting cheese. I mean, you've only known her, what? A month?"

"And a half. But we connected in Tampa three

years ago and I've known her from Twitter for a while."

"It's still probably better to end things now if it means she gets a decent job and people are only talking about how great her writing sample was."

"Shit. You're right."

"You're gonna have to be the bad guy, Owen."

"Yeah, I know… I got this."

FRANKIE

I'm just going to say it: I hate Vegas.

It's my understanding that Las Vegas is an extremely popular destination for travelers between the ages of twenty-one and thirty-four, but as an individual who is chronologically aged smack-dab in the middle of that horrible demographic, I can safely say that what happens here can stay here because I want nothing to do with it. It's the exact opposite of everything I can tolerate in this world. If I ever make it big as a stand-up comic, I will just turn down all invitations to perform here. I don't care if everyone does Vegas. Frankie Hogan doesn't do Vegas. I mean, unless I have to accompany Owen and Sam here again. Then I'll do it begrudgingly.

I could totally see Sam and me having a blast in Atlantic City though. Playing bingo and eating at some crappy buffet until we can't sit up. Not when we're senior citizens, but now. We had a pretty great time in this hotel suite all day. I did miss Owen, but Sam is great company and the movie channel and minibar selections are top-notch.

Sam is sleeping so soundly, I wonder if Owen and I can just sneak over to my room for a quickie. Owen and I have gotten really good at sexting lately, but our text conversations are starting to use up most of the memory on my phone. For that and other reasons, we need to have some actual physical contact ASAP. Although it definitely wouldn't be worth it if Sam was kidnapped while we were getting it on. So we'd better keep it in our pants. I'll just delete some apps from my phone to make room for more sexting and hope that once the tour is over, Owen and I can have some more alone time together.

Although I might only have time to see him if he comes to visit me while I'm waiting tables at whatever eating establishment is dumb enough to hire me. The job market is very sad right now for people like me. And by "people like me" I mean underappreciated geniuses of comedy who hate taking orders from people in offices and don't want to take orders and carry them to and from people in restaurants either.

It's possible I might need an attitude adjustment.

Or a miracle.

If I could somehow work on Owen's show, I

think my life might become unrecognizably perfect. Not that it's my dream job, but it would be amazing to get a writer's assistant gig. It would be my first legit Hollywood job after three years. I would rock that shit. It's not like being a regular assistant. It's not secretarial work, and I wouldn't be picking up people's dry cleaning. I'd be in the writers' room while they're breaking stories. Yeah, I'd be typing up notes on my laptop all day so I can summarize what everyone said during the story meetings. But I'd be in the room, working for the showrunner, and if I'm lucky I'd get to pitch ideas and maybe even co-write an episode. It's an entry-level position, but that's better than no level at all! I would learn so much.

It's about time for Owen to get back, so I run to the bathroom to check myself out in the mirror. Such a girly move, and I don't even feel bad about it. I want him to have the best possible memory of what I look like when I leave him to go back to my room so we can write dirty texts to each other until we fall asleep.

When I hear the door to the suite open, I get so excited it's almost embarrassing.

I run out of the bathroom and smash into him, wrapping my arms around him and burying my face in his chest. He smells like Las Vegas, and that doesn't even bother me. "Hi. Hi. Hi. Hi. Hi," I whisper.

It takes him a few seconds, but he finally puts his

arms around me too. "Hey," he says, patting me on the back. He sounds tired.

I look up at him. "You okay?"

He nods. "Long day." He lets go of me and continues walking into the living room area. "He asleep?"

"Yep. Out like a light, last time I checked."

It's a two-bedroom suite. Owen goes into Sam's room to give him a goodnight kiss—something he does every night. He doesn't look at me when he comes out, closing the door. He goes to the minibar to pour himself a shot of whiskey, which is odd. He gulps it down, which is really odd. He doesn't ask me if I want any, which is just rude, but I don't want any, so whatever.

He goes over to plop down on the sofa, combing his fingers through his hair.

"How was your show?"

"It was good." He pats the cushion next to him. "Let's talk for a minute, if you have time."

"I have time." I resist the urge to straddle him, sit down next to him on the sofa, and clasp my hands on my lap. "What's up?"

"I have good news," he says, as if he's about to tell me bad news. "I just got an email from Barry Weiner, the producer of the sitcom."

"*The Untitled Nanny Project*, you mean?" I joke.

He rubs his forehead. "Yeah, we really need to come up with a title for that shit. Anyway, I got an email from Barry. He and the showrunner loved your writing sample."

"Really? Cool." I prepare myself for the next bit of news, which I'm assuming is: *but they can't hire you because you lack experience.*

"They want you on staff as the writer's assistant."

I do a cartoon doubletake. "What? Shut up. That's not funny."

"They really do. Normally you'd have to meet with them so they can decide if they want you in the room with them every day or not. But I vouched for you." He studies my face. "Are you interested?"

"Of course I'm interested. Seriously? They want to hire me. Like, now, you mean?"

He stares down at his right knee, draws circles around it with his fingertip. "To start in a few weeks. Hopefully you'll be able to pay your bills until then. I'd be happy to just give you whatever you need until your first paycheck."

"No, I'll be fine. I think. So when we're back in LA in a few days, I'm done being Sam's nanny, right? Just confirming."

Owen nods without looking at me. "He'll be with Ashley for a couple of weeks straight, so Blanca will take care of him."

"Right."

"So, you want the writer's assistant job? For the sitcom? Just to confirm."

"Yes! You should call your show *Funny Business*.

That works, right? He's a comedian. The kids are funny. The nanny is hilarious. There's no funny business between him and the nanny, at least not for the first season." I give him an exaggerated wink.

He finally looks at me again. "Shit. That's good. That's perfect."

"I know! I'm awesome! I can't thank you enough for this job, Owen." I lean in to hug him, but he pulls away and holds his hand up.

His hand touches my boob, but not in the good way. He's pushing me away. Literally and figuratively.

"I'm glad you want the job. It'll be really good for you. You'll learn a lot. The showrunner's a good guy. He won't make you get everyone coffee or anything like that. He'll actually want to hear your ideas. It'll be great for the show too. We need a funny asshole on the writing staff. Most family comedy writers are way too nice."

His delivery was good, and I might have laughed if he hadn't just blocked my hug.

I sit back, away from him. "Happy to be of service."

"The thing is, it's not a good idea for us to see each other anymore if you're going to be working for me. With me. On the same show as me. In the room with all those other writers who are writing for me."

"You mean not a good idea for people to know we're seeing each other?"

He looks me dead straight in the eyes. "It's just not a good idea for us to see each other outside of work. While we're working together. Other than as friends."

It feels like the air conditioning suddenly came on full blast. But maybe it's a freezing gust from Owen Brodie revealing his true nature and ice-cold heart. The words *I love you* are crystalizing and swirling all around me and then crashing into the words *as friends*, smashing into a million tiny pieces.

"As *friends*...? So let me get this straight. You're breaking up with me. Not that we were ever officially anything, but if I take this job on your show, we will definitely never officially be anything."

"I'm not saying never. Just not while we're working together. It's for your own good."

"Hah! Certainly feels that way. I'm feeling really good right now. Like a load has been lifted. A giant load of cocky asshole."

"I understand if you're mad."

"Do ya?"

"I mean, I'd rather you be mad at me than sad about it."

"Fantastic. Great to know. Everything's going exactly the way you want it to, then."

"Trust me, this isn't the way I want things to go

for us, Frankie." He leans toward me, but I stand up and start pacing around.

Tears sting my eyes, but I refuse to cry in front of him.

"So…what? Are we going to lie to everyone on the show about knowing each other? They'll find out that I opened for you in Detroit."

"No, of course not. They can know that you were Sam's nanny while I was on tour."

"And of course they'll all just assume we never got involved. Because how could you possibly be interested in someone like me?"

"If anyone asks if we were involved, I'll be called upon to do the most serious acting of my career. What do you mean 'someone like you'? Frankie… You're—"

I hold up my hand to make him stop talking because all I heard was "if we were involved." Past tense. We're already past tense. "Just…don't." I don't want to hear whatever it is he's about to say right now. I just need to know one thing. I have to clear the lump from my throat before lowering my voice and saying, "I promised Sam I'd take him to the Wizarding World of Harry Potter at Universal Studios before school starts."

"You can still do that. You can see Sam whenever you want. I want to make this as easy on him as possible. He's really going to miss having you around."

"You can't imagine how much I'm going to miss him."

"We're all still going to see each other, Frankie. This isn't the end of the world." He gets up and walks toward me, reaching out for me.

I back away from him. "It's the end of the world that I actually liked living in."

Drop the mic.

I have to leave the room after a line like that.

I don't even know where that came from. What kind of drama queen says things like that? Not me.

I've probably just been indoors for too long. Too much recycled air. Way too many stupid feelings.

I have no idea what to do once I'm in my own room.

I can't sleep.

I can't drink when I'm still on the job.

I don't have Mia or my other girlfriends around to force me to get dressed up and go out and get hammered so I can get over my latest disastrous non-relationship.

I just have to lie here and be sad. So, so sad.

I feel so stupid. I let myself fall for Owen so hard. There was no other way for me to fall for him. I should have just closed off my heart completely. He's the guy in the pictures on my wall, and I'm the Tampa Heckler. I should have known there was no way this would work.

The only way this works is if he's the ridiculously

handsome celebrity that I make fun of because I'm so mad at him for not wanting me.

I can do that.

I've done it before; I'll do it again.

At least this time I'll have a decent job while I'm doing it.

I have to see Sam and Owen in the morning and travel with them to San Francisco and then to Los Angeles. And that will be the end of this nanny job. I'll eat breakfast with them and hang out at airports with them. I'll read Harry Potter with Sam and stay on Cheese Watch before flights. I'll do all of it knowing that what happened between Owen and me in New York and Detroit and Texas and all those other cities is going to stay there. But what just happened here—that's what I get to take with me back to LA.

Yeah.

I really hate Vegas.

OWEN

One Mostly Shitty Month Later

"Hello, Owen? Is this Owen Brodie the so-called comedian who's doin' a show about a single dad with a bunch of cute kids and a nanny? This is Fran Drescher, honey. Star of the beloved 90s television hit *The Nanny*. Maybe ya heard of it? Ahhhhahaha-hahaha. I heard you broke up with that sweet thing Frankie Hogan last week, *mistah*. And I just want you to know that I saw her the other day, all right? She's fine. We had a cuppa *cawffee*, we got our nails done, we talked it out; she's over it. Trust me, honey—I know from a *meshugeneh*, and this girl is very classy, with the *savoir faire* and the sophistication, and she's no schmo. So. She's ready to go to work on Monday, and you have nothin' to worry about, all right? You're a real mensch for gettin' her this job, and she only thinks about your schlong around ten or twenty times a day now... Shit."

And that's when she hung up. I've listened to that message ten or twenty times a day for the past few weeks. I called the number back and discovered she'd called from a Texas barbecue restaurant in North Hollywood. We'd talked about going there together, after visiting my parents, so that really hurt. But I'll never delete that message.

I'm also never going to delete the voicemail that immediately followed it...

"Hi hi hey hey hi, Owen Brodie, this is Amy Poehler. Listen, I'm here with Fran Drescher, and I just wanted you to know that what she said about Frankie Hogan—who is a living legend and one of the most talented and underrated comedians of our time, and she's incredible—what Fran said was mostly true, but she made up that last part because she's drunk and insane and off her meds. Not really though—please don't sue—haha! Love you, Fran Drescher! So I just want to clarify that the wildly talented and brilliantly beautiful Frankie Hogan does *not* think about your wiener more than five times a day, tops. So if you could just slightly get over yourself just a teeny tiny bit, Mr. Owen Brodie, that would be fabulous, thank you so much. Bye-bye!"

And also *this* voicemail from a burner phone that she has either disposed of or is simply ignoring my calls from...

"Hellooooo, Owen?! This is Drew Barrymore! I am so excited to pass along this amazing message from one of my very favorite people in the entire universe—Frankie Hogan! She is the most beautiful, hilarious flower I have ever had the amazing pleasure to know, and I just want to tell you that she has blossomed. Absolutely and totally blossomed in the past few weeks as a writer's assistant on your show. So thank you so, so much for blessing her and believing in her enough to hire her for that job, even though you don't think she's special enough to be your girlfriend. It's absolutely totally fine and beautiful because it, like, wasn't cosmically aligned or whatever, and that's completely okay!

"She's going to morning spin classes when she's only a little bit hungover, and she's reading my absolute favorite book, *Eat, Pray, Love*. She told me it's the funniest thing she's ever read, so that's obviously amazing. Anyway, I just wanted you to know how amazing Frankie's doing, so you definitely shouldn't feel bad about being such a shithead loser dickbrain when you visited the *Funny Business* writers' room yesterday, okay? She completely understands that you had to act like you've never had your face up in her yoni business, but you could have been, like, maybe eighty-five percent less of an asshole when other people were around.

"She wasn't embarrassed or anything—everything's super beautiful. She just thinks you were a little bit cold for someone who once told her you loved her and almost cried that time when you ejaculated inside her. But like I said, she totally gets that you did it for her own good, and she appreciates it so much. So thank you, Owen Brodie and the universe! 'Kay, bye."

Yeah, that was my bad.

I had a meeting with the writing staff the other day, and I was so excited to see Frankie. I had tried calling and texting her to check in and see how she's doing, but she never answered. She took Sam to Universal Studios when he was staying with Ashley, so I never got to see her.

I get it, it's fine.

I didn't want to be a pathetic schmo when I saw her at work, so I went the other way. I was cold. It's what I did back in Vegas. I figured it's easier for her to be mad at me than to be sad. But I'm miserable when I'm home alone. It actually *is* pathetic. It's weird not having her around.

I would do nothing but lie in bed watching her YouTube videos and eating ice cream from the container if I didn't have to stay in shape for the TV show.

If she wasn't so mad at me—if she wasn't being

such a little turd—I'd try to work things out with her. Barry and the showrunner have been so impressed with her. She's been kicking ass as a writer's assistant. Everyone else on the staff loves her. Surely they wouldn't care if they found out we were dating. Or maybe people would care, but you know what? Fuck 'em.

I just don't know if Frankie will ever forgive me for ending things with her.

I don't know if Sam will ever forgive me either.

Mama unfollowed me on Twitter for two hours when she found out—I only know this because she texted to tell me she unfollowed me and then she texted to tell me she felt guilty so she followed me again. But she only retweets Frankie now and she never "likes" *my* tweets.

I slip my phone back into my pocket so I can pay for Sam's frozen yogurt. It only took him ten minutes to load up on toppings, and I swear he just chose the heaviest ones because he thinks he can punish me by making me pay more. *Bring it on, kid. Pile on those brownie bites. I can take it.* He wasn't even excited to come here. He isn't excited about anything anymore. Not even cheese.

Lady Hilarious McFunnyPants really did take all the sunshine with her.

She doesn't even at-reply my tweets anymore.

I feel so alone.

"You want to sit over here?" I ask my son. He's

wearing his private school uniform, and he's already managed to get chocolate syrup on it. He did that on purpose too, I'll bet, because I'm the one who'll have to wash it this weekend.

Well played, Samuel Brodie. Well played.

He shrugs. "I guess."

I take a seat at one of the tables by the window, and he takes a seat at the table next to me.

"Oh, that's funny," I tell him. "You sure that's far enough away from me? I can still talk to you from over here."

"I won't listen though," he says. And then he practically unhinges his jaw so he can fit a giant spoonful of brownie bites into his mouth. When his mouth is full, he chews spitefully but without passion, while glaring at me.

"So you like your new teacher?"

He shrugs and nods.

I pick up the extra spoon and hold it like a microphone. "Great! Thanks for coming out tonight! Hey, what did the booger say to the teacher?"

Sam blinks at me, shaking his head. I know he knows the answer to this fantastic joke, but he's pretending not to, just to be a jerk.

"That's right! He said 'Pick me!' And you're loving your classmates, am I right?"

He grunts.

I've had tougher crowds than this, little turd. A drunk guy once threw his cowboy boot at me in Memphis. His prosthetic leg was still in it. You'll have to do better than that.

"Hey, do you know if there's a school for garbage collectors?"

He ignores me, stabs at the brownies, and takes another bite.

"You are absolutely right! There isn't a school for garbage collectors—you just pick it up as you go along!"

Absolutely no acknowledgment of my existence.

"What did the right butt cheek say to the left butt cheek?"

I see a twitch of recognition. A tiny indication that this child is willing to accept—maybe not that I'm his father and he loves me—but that I'm alive and in the room with him, if only so he can find out what one butt cheek said to the other.

"What?" he mumbles.

"'If we work together, we can stop this crap.'"

Sam's face cheeks work together to try to stop him from laughing, but no muscle in his seven-year-old-boy body is strong enough to fight a reaction to a poop joke. He laughs, and melted frozen yogurt drips out of his mouth. It's a glorious sight.

I pick up a napkin and wipe his chin.

"Glad you liked that one. Poop jokes aren't my favorite jokes. But they are number two."

Now he's in stitches. Tiny brownie particles are spraying everywhere, and I'm king of the world.

This is literally the high point of the past month for me. I feel like slightly less of a dickhead in this moment, as I wipe my son's chocolate-y saliva from my own face.

When he's stopped laughing and swallowing, I finally say the thing that I've been wanting to say to him: "You miss Frankie, don't you?"

He glances over at me, frowning, and then looks away. "Yes."

"I do too."

"Then why isn't she here?"

"Because she has another job to do. She's not your nanny anymore."

He lets go of his spoon and huffs. "She wasn't *just* my nanny."

"What do you mean?"

He better not say she was my shower buddy.

"She's the only person who made you smile and laugh. You're always trying to make other people laugh, but she was the only one who ever made you smile with your eyes and laugh with your whole face."

"That's not true. You've always made me smile and laugh. Ever since you were born."

He shakes his head vehemently. "Not like Frankie. You're always worried when you look at me. I make you worried. Frankie made you happy. So happy you didn't even care how weird you look when you laugh really hard."

"Wait a minute. I look weird when I laugh really hard?"

That response would have made Frankie try really hard not to laugh, but my son doesn't get my hot-guy humor. Which is fine.

"Yeah, your face gets weird. It's weird seeing all your teeth."

"Well, I'm learning a lot about myself right now, so thanks."

He stares at me while taking a careful bite of frozen yogurt and then says, "What did my dumb dad say to my nanny to make her leave?" It takes me a second to realize this is supposed to be a joke, but before I can respond, he says, "Nothing. He didn't talk to her about stuff like he was supposed to, as usual."

"What? How do you know that?"

"I heard Frankie talking to Mom."

"What? When?"

"When she brought me back from Harry Potter."

"Your mom was talking to Frankie about me?" I don't know why this surprises me, since I've been dreading it ever since I emailed Frankie about coming on the tour with us. I've pictured my ex-wife sitting down with every woman I've been attracted to since the divorce, like it's a talk show and she's the host who's listening to them discuss what they like about me and then she tells them exactly what's wrong with me and how I'll disappoint them.

That would actually be a great fantasy sequence for *Funny Business*... I need to remember that.

"What did she say?"

He sighs. "Nothing bad, Dad. Mom doesn't say bad stuff about you when you aren't around."

"She doesn't?"

He shakes his head. "She got Frankie talking because she could tell something was making everyone sad. They were in the kitchen, and they didn't think I could hear them. Frankie told her about the job you got her, for writing, but you don't want people to know that you liked each other. Mom rolled her eyes and said you should have talked about what Frankie wants. With Frankie."

"Well, it's awfully ironic that she's telling Frankie this and not me."

He blinks twice and then says, "I still don't know what *ironic* means."

"Yeah, I still don't know how to explain what it means. But trust me—that was ironic."

"Mom just said you probably were talking to your boys when you should have been talking to Frankie. But she also told Frankie that you were really sad ever since we came back."

"Were you spying on them, buddy? You heard a lot."

He shrugs. "People think I don't pay attention just because I don't talk a lot. It's easy. People can be dumb like that." He looks down at his dessert. "*Fro-yo* information, I gotta eat this before it melts now."

I fucking love this kid so much.

"Yeah. You do that. Thanks for the talk."

"You're welcome, Dad. You'll be okay."

Crap.

I can tell jokes on stage despite having things thrown at me, but I can't seem to say three little words when my nose is tingling and I have a stupid lump in my throat.

So I lean over to muss up his hair.

We'll be okay.

FRANKIE

"Hello, Miss Hogan. This is Maxwell Sheffield from 90s TV sitcom *The Nanny*—which is surprisingly humorous but in no way the inspiration for future streaming sitcom sensation *Funny Business*. It has been brought to my attention that fellow thespian Owen Brodie, who is otherwise of sound mind and fine character, has perhaps been a bit of an arse regarding a certain personal and professional matter for the past month. He would like to know if you are open to returning to a relationship of a loving and intimate nature with him and if you would then be comfortable with him alerting people to the fact that he is, and I quote, 'giving you the hot beef injection.' He believes that since you have been performing at such a high level as a writer's assistant that surely only an idiot would believe you got any job simply because you're somebody's niece or somebody's love muffin. The truth is he misses everything about you, all the time. Including, but not limited to, being balls deep in your delicious fanny. He would like me to point out that he means *fanny* in the British sense. Not the American one. Because no butt stuff. Please respond at your convenience. But very quickly."

I look over at Mia, who's clutching her heart and pouting. It's the first time I've let her hear that voice-mail. I myself have now heard it seventeen times.

"Awwww. Frankie. That's the cutest message I've ever heard. You have to call him back!"

"Hang on, there's another one."

I play her the next voicemail on speakerphone too. This one's in Owen's regular voice.

"Hey, I just want to clarify that I had never really seen *The Nanny* until an hour ago when I watched a bunch of clips on YouTube. So if my Maxwell impression was a little off—that's why. And also because I'm not as good at impressions as you are. But get over yourself. But it's actually a pretty funny show. I was surprised. But call me back."

"Frankie!" She jumps up and down. "Call him back call him back call him back! When did he leave those messages?"

"A couple of days ago. He also sent a text yesterday."

I show her the text message.

OWEN: *I know I screwed up. I just need to know that I*

can try to make this up to you. Give me the green light. If not, I'll back off. But I miss you. Sam misses you. My schlong misses you.

OWEN: *That felt all kinds of wrong, writing Sam and schlong in the same text.*

OWEN: *Shit. Did it again.*

OWEN: *Let me know.*

Mia looks like she's about to have an actual breakdown. "Frankie! What are you waiting for?! You've been so sad. Just give him the green light. You don't mind people at work knowing you're dating, right?"

"I mean. They seem pretty cool. But who knows how they'd react. I mean, if I pitch a story idea and get to write it, somebody might think I only got the chance because I'm getting the hot beef injection from the star of the show."

"Yeah, but some jealous asshole is always going to think something bad no matter what. That's not just show business—that's any business."

"Wow. That's the most cynical thing you've ever said. I love it."

"Well, it's not even cynical unfortunately. That's just the way the world works. Ohhhh, call him! Text him! Do something!"

"I have to get ready for a show tonight. I need to get into performance mode. I already have my set worked out, and I need to get into that headspace."

She pouts again. She's very good at it. But not good enough.

"I have to get ready."

She huffs. "Fine!"

I get a notification on my phone. It's from Twitter. I have a direct message from Owen Brodie.

OWEN BRODIE: *I know you have a show tonight, so you're probably busy. I'm dying over here, baby. Just give me a sign.*

Mia watches me staring at my phone. Perhaps it's the tiny high-pitched kitten-like sound I make that tips her off as to what I'm reading. "He sent you another text, didn't he?"

"Twitter DM."

I mean, I don't want him to die over this or anything. Especially since he called me "baby."

ME: *<winking face emoji>*

I put my phone on Silent Mode, then place it on top of my dresser, facedown, and start to get ready for my show at the comedy club on Sunset.

"Yayyyyy." Mia claps her hands. "I'm so excited for you. I'll go charge my phone so I can record your act."

"Thank you. You're the actual best, Mia."

She smiles and shrugs as she walks out. "I know."

About two minutes later, I hear her yelling from her room. "Frankie! Frankie! Check your Twitter! Check your Twitter!"

I do.

I check my Twitter.

I've been at-mentioned.

Owen Brodie @theowenbrodie

I ducking love you, @frankiesayrelax . But don't let it go to your head or anything ;)

What a maniac.

That tweet has already been "liked" and retweeted by Mia and Mama Brodie.

And gotten over five hundred likes total.

I have no idea how to respond to this, so I just "like" the tweet and put my phone away again.

I can't walk into a twenty-one-and-over comedy club and tell jokes about my screwed-up love life with a big dumb grin on my face! That's not my style. I might have to change my style eventually—soon, even. But not yet.

I am not, in fact, going to let this go to my head.

It's going to my heart and my lady bits but not my head.

I know I've performed for nearly two thousand people in a theater, but this is my first time being a part of an official comedy lineup in LA. I'm nervous. Not bad-nervous, but I have the pre-show jitters, and that's a good thing. All comedians get them, I've heard, no matter how long they've been doing this for. The guy who was on before me killed—and I'm happy for him—but I also hate him a little bit because he got the crowd a little too warmed up. What if they're tired of laughing already?

The owner of the club signals at me to get ready to take the stage, but I'm ready.

The host finishes up his bit. "And ever since then, our safe word has been: '*seriously?*' Ladies and gentlemen, this is the first time our next comic is performing on the Comedy Shop stage. She hails from Tampa, Florida, she's performed to a sold-out crowd in Detroit, she's the writer's assistant on a forthcoming sitcom called *Funny Business*, and she drove herself here all the way from Pico Boulevard. Let's give a warm but mildly sarcastic welcome to the very amusing Frankie Hogan."

I get a pretty good round of applause from the audience as my ukulele and I take the stage. The whole interior of this place is painted black and there are spotlights in my eyes, so I can hardly see the audience from here, but it looked pretty full when I was waiting over by the bar. I know Mia is out there, of course. I can still hear her yelling out my name and *woohoo*-ing.

Right before the applause dies down, I pick up the mic and launch right into it. "Hello, Comedy Shop audience! I love this location because I can stop by Target *and* Pink Taco on the way home. What a great-looking crowd of people that I can't see at all because of the lights in my eyes. It's Los Angeles, so I can safely assume that you're all hot."

From the back of the room, a man yells out with a slightly muffled voice, "You got that right!"

"Well now, someone thinks pretty highly of himself. Good for you, sir!"

"You think pretty highly of myself too, baby!" he says.

Shit.

I know that voice.

My heart and my lady bits know that voice.

But my head will stay in the game.

"Gotta love those cocky hot guys. Speaking of pink tacos and Target—anyone here ever been *so* attracted to someone even though you know it couldn't possibly work out with them, but you're like, 'Let's just have sex one time to get each other out of our systems'?"

There's plenty of clapping and hollering.

"Sure, a lot of us have said that. Let's hear from those of you who've had sex with someone you're super attracted to one time and actually gotten them out of your systems…"

Laughter and no applause.

"Yeah, that's because it's like walking into Target and saying you're just going to buy *the one thing* on your shopping list."

"I fucking love that joke!" Owen yells out from the back of the room. "You're brilliant!"

What is he doing?

Reverse-heckling me?

"Keep going!" he calls out, clapping. "You're doing great!"

He knows the owner of this club. He's performed here tons of times. No one's going to tell him to shut up. I can actually hear some ladies giggling, probably because they can see him.

"You're ruining my set, sir!" I say into the mic.

"No I'm not! We make comedy magic happen— keep going!"

"I just forgot all the bits I had planned!"

"Do anything! Do your mum's joke suggestions! They'll kill!"

I'm going to kill him.

Is he drunk?

He doesn't sound drunk.

"This is very weird, *Owen*."

"I fucking love you, Frankie Hogan, and so will everyone else—just say anything!" I can hear him getting closer.

"Fine!" My love-addled brain somehow manages to find what I'm looking for, so I pull my phone out, pretending to read from it, and I do my most recent Donna Hogan joke suggestions, even though I wasn't planning on doing them tonight.

They actually do kill.

I can hear Owen yelping from about ten feet away now. "I love your mum, and I can't wait for her to be my mother-in-law!"

Whaaaaat?

"Too soon?" he says.

"No, she would totally marry you!" Mia yells out.

"If you propose to me during my first set at the Comedy Shop, I will never speak to you again."

"Fair enough!" he says. "Sing a cute, funny song now, babe. You got this."

"Yeah, I was going to sing a cute, funny song now and I know I've got this. Thanks."

I put the mic back on the stand and pick up my uke.

This guy is out of his mind.

But I'm not going to let him derail my act.

I got this.

"This is a little song I wrote before the person I wrote the song about actually became the thing that I said I was hoping he'd become in the song... But now, all of a sudden, he's back to *not* being that thing anymore—sort of. But I guess that also means he's actually being the thing that I said I wanted him to be, so… Never mind! Please enjoy this song."

I pluck at a few strings on the ukulele and then sing in a raspy Bonnie Tyler-type voice.

"Be a dick…
Every now and then I get a little uninspired
And I blame it all on you
Be a dick…
Every now and then I get a little uncomfortable
Because you're being so nice to me
Be a dick…
Every now and then I get a little bit angry
That you aren't the dickhead I thought you'd be
Be a dick…
Every now and then I get so pissed off you're around
'Cuz now I can't even compartmentalize
Be a dick, Blue Eyes
Stop being so damn good to all my lady parts
Be a dick, Blue Eyes
Seriously how am I supposed to write a funny song about
our breakup if you're being so awesome?

Once upon a time my love life was a joke
But now I'm filling two shopping carts
There's nothing I can sing
Total eclipse of the fart…jokes
Once upon a time there were dicks in my life
But now there's just a beautiful cock

There's nothing to complain about
Total eclipse of the fart...jokes."

I had a couple more verses written, but I think this audience has gotten enough entertainment from my love life tonight, and I don't think I can wait two more minutes before running off this stage into Owen Brodie's arms.

Or possibly running off the stage to slap his stupid obnoxious handsome face.

I haven't decided yet.

Either way, he'd better brace himself.

OWEN

I once got tackled by a three-hundred-pound drunk guy who tried to hug me after a show in Little Rock, back when I was just starting out in stand-up. He was really nice and complimentary. It was surprisingly awesome, really. But being tackled by Frankie Hogan after she ran off stage just now was better.

She was mad and happy, and people were clapping and hollering.

I could tell she didn't know if she wanted to kiss me or strangle me.

But she settled on hugging me, and it was great.

And now I've brought her back to the owner's office so I can talk to her in private. Her hand is warm, but I can feel her trembling. She's still got the performance jitters. Or maybe she's just excited to see me. Either way, it's cute and I can't stop touching her.

"Is Sam with Ashley tonight?" she asks.

"I love that you asked that. Yes. I told him I was coming to see you though."

"Is it okay for us to be back here?"

"I talked to the owner before I came tonight. It's fine."

"Baller... Although this room does not smell great."

"No kidding. This is where I was when I realized I'd have to hire a nanny for the tour. After Sam barfed up all the dessert I let him eat right before bringing him here for my set."

"Awww. I heard about that. Poor thing."

"I got over it. Wasn't that hard to clean up."

"I was talking about Sam."

"Right. That's one of the many reasons why I don't think you're terrible. Or one of the least terrible things about you, I should say. You care about my son so much."

"I love your son so much."

"I love that you love my son so much."

She punches my bicep. "I've really, really missed seeing him every day."

"I know. He misses you too. You were great out there, by the way. So funny and so cute." I kiss her forehead.

I can tell she wants to complain about how condescending that is, but she holds her tongue and says, "Thank you. It was fun."

320

"They loved you. Everyone does." I kiss her left cheek. "I talked to Marty tonight." I kiss her right cheek.

"Don't call him Marty."

"I told him I want to start seeing you again. I told him that I want people to know we're in a relationship and that I will say and do whatever I have to—to make it clear that you were hired as a writer's assistant based on your sense of humor and talent. That any success that comes your way is because of who you are. Not because of who you're schtupping." I kiss her sweet, quivering lips. "Is that okay with you?"

"Yes."

"Good. Because I want to call the *Funny Business* guys tomorrow to tell them. Is that also okay with you?"

She rests her forehead against my chest. "Yes."

"Good. This isn't an easy career we've chosen, but if we stick together, I think we'll be okay."

She nods and makes a little kitty cat sound.

"By the way, I think Martin might have a crush on your roommate because he asked if I've met her and if I can set him up with her."

"Unacceptable. Absolutely not."

"Fair enough." She's exactly the right amount of annoyed and adorable right now, so I pull something out of my jacket pocket. "Hey. Why do melons have to have weddings?"

She looks up at me, confused for a second, and then I watch as she realizes it's a corny joke. "Because they cantaloupe."

"Hey, that's right." I hold up the little velvet box between us.

Her jaw drops, even as she grabs it from me. "Are you out of your fucking mind?!"

"I did tell you that you drive me insane, but I'm not actually out of my mind, no."

She opens the box and finds the very tastefully designed promise ring in there.

"It's a promise ring, not an engagement ring. I don't even know your birthday month, so I got one with Sam's birthstone. I figured we should probably celebrate at least one birthday together before getting engaged."

She seems so relieved, even as she slides the ring onto her left ring finger. "Good."

"This is just to show you and everyone else that I love you and I'm serious about you."

"Uh-huh."

"You don't even have to move in with me right away."

"Now you're talkin'!" She twists her lips to the side. "I mean, I wouldn't *mind* living with you. Especially when Sam's there."

"Wow. Take it down a notch, will you? I can only take so much adoration."

"Well, that's too bad because I'm sensing a lot of

adoration coming your way tonight." She starts kissing me all over my face. "I don't know if you'll be able to handle it."

"I think I can handle you." I give her ass a squeeze. "We should probably go back to my place to do the adoring though. The sofa in here is nasty."

She cups her ear, pretending she didn't hear me. "Come again?"

We know all the same jokes, and our timing is perfect.

"Exactly. And a few yogurt stains too."

EPILOGUE ONE

MAMA BRODIE: *Is my girl all moved in yet?*

FRANKIE: *One more box of old joke notebooks and he's all done carrying my stuff in. Fortunately, my jokes are very light. For instance: How many pretty-boy comedians does it take to change a lightbulb? There's only one pretty-boy comedian, and he changes all lightbulbs as soon as they burn out because he wants to make sure everyone can always see how pretty he is.*

MAMA BRODIE: *Ahahahahaaaaa!!! I just spat my drink out on my shirt!*

POPS BRODIE: *Let me wipe that up for you, darlin'.*

MAMA BRODIE: *Oh my, Mr. Brodie. Use a towel next time. <winking face emoji>*

OWEN: *That lightbulb joke could use a little editing, babe. But I actually want all the lights to work so I can always see YOU ;)*

FRANKIE: *Awww. We're all so ducking adorable. I love us. I wish Sam had a phone.*

DYLAN: *Could you guys keep your ducking adorable couples text conversations to yourselves? Some of us are single again over here.*

MILES: *I knew it. You all owe me ten bucks. Each.*

POPS BRODIE: *Pretty sure you all owe ME twenty bucks each. I had *breakup the day after the show closes**

MILES: *You're right. Can I Venmo you?*

POPS BRODIE: *You know it.*

FRANKIE: *I'm really sorry it didn't work out, Dylan*

DYLAN: *Thank you, non-asshole person who isn't related to me by blood.*

OWEN: *I am also really sorry it didn't work out, Dylan.*

DYLAN: *Thank you, nicer brother who's only being nice because his girlfriend is nice.*

OWEN: *She's not that nice.*

FRANKIE: *It's true. I'm not.*

DYLAN: *In other news, my shrink has just informed me that he's retiring and I'll have to start over with someone new. So that is also fucking awesome.*

MAMA BRODIE: *Oh, sugar. I'm so sorry about all of it. Why don't you just come stay with us for a spell before going back to LA? I will make aaalllllll the chocolate pecan pies you can eat.*

DYLAN: *I actually have to do a commercial in a couple of weeks so I can't eat my feelings. But thanks. Also, I'm gonna try to win her back. I think she still loves me.*

MILES: *Who had *immediately tries to win her back and isn't even ashamed of it* ?*

OWEN: *That was me. I prefer Zelle to Venmo or PayPal now, thanks.*

DYLAN: *I can't wait to tell my next therapist about all of you.*

FRANKIE: *My best friend actually has a really great therapist if you need a recommendation.*

FRANKIE: *Actually, never mind.*

OWEN: *Mia is the most well-adjusted person I've ever met. Besides Sam. Give him the info.*

FRANKIE: *It's just that Mia's always talking about how beautiful her therapist is. But she is prone to exaggeration.*

OWEN: *Never mind.*

MILES: *That's a HELL NO. I can get you some names, bro.*

DYLAN: *Hook me up, Frankie. She sounds perfect for me.*

EPILOGUE TWO - FRANKIE HOGAN JOKE NOTEBOOK

THE WEDDING VOWS EDITION

Owen,

I spent the last month writing and rewriting vows in my joke notebook.

Some of the crap I came up with was actually pretty funny.

But it didn't capture how I feel about marrying you.

So I decided to start over and just write from the heart.

I'll use the other stuff in future episodes of the international hit streaming sitcom sensation Funny Business *and give all the best lines to the beloved side character I play, of course. The stuff that's not about your* best man, *I mean (exaggerated wink). But as a staff writer, I will continue to fight the good fight against the executives over the use of creative schlong terms. Because the family comedy–viewing audience is ready for a side of hot beef injection with their fart jokes.*

It was two years ago that you gave me the promise

ring to wear. You said it was so people would know we're a couple. It was a lovely ring and a lovely sentiment. But from that night on, nobody has needed to see a ring on my finger to understand how much you care about me. Not even me. You have been relentless in your pursuit to include me in every discussion about every decision that affects us and Sam and most of the ones that only affect you. But anything that affects you affects me, you keep reminding me.

And while I may never forgive you for convincing me to allow you to set my uncle up with my best friend—because that is just weird and every kind of wrong—they are, in fact, very cute together.

But not as cute as we are—which is also just weird and every kind of wrong.

You went from being the pretty-boy model on my wall to the pretty-boy comedian on my Twitter feed to the father of my favorite kid to the best lover and boyfriend I've ever had to the greatest love of my life.

At first, there was so much I tried to hold back because I was afraid of losing myself to you. But the truth is you somehow allowed me to become more Me for you and Sam. For better or for worse. For richer or for poorer. In sickness and in health. To love and to heckle and to cherish...

I guess I can change your contact name from Asshole Fiancé *on my phone to* Asshole Husband *tonight. Because* Asshole Fatherofmyfavoritekidandunbornspawn *is too many characters.*

I promise to always give you and Sam everything I have and to always take whatever you have to offer and make it funnier and more tolerable.

As always, I did some Google research on how to write a wedding vow, and one website advised against using words like always *and* never.

Fuck that.

I will love you forever. I will always be your closest companion, your biggest fan, your worst critic, your most enthusiastic audience, your greatest champion, your most passionate lover, and your most reliable friend.

And I never, ever want to write a breakup song about you.

With this ring, I thee wed.

I'm your fucking wife now, Head Shot.

But get over yourself.

EPILOGUE THREE - OWEN
BRODIE JOKE NOTEBOOK

THE WEDDING VOWS EDITION

Frankie,

This isn't going to be very funny.

My life with you—the life we've created so far, the life we will be creating together—it's fun and it's funny, but it's no joke. It's something I take very seriously. Always have. Always will.

Comedians, as you know, are like philosophers. We're funny philosophers. But we overthink everything and try to make light of everything because if we don't we're just sad, confused people who have no control over anything. You're my favorite subject to overthink about. I also enjoy observing myself in relation to you. More than anyone, you've helped to shape my identity and my voice and my delivery—as a comedian and as a man.

I can't say that I ever felt lost, exactly. Or maybe I did and I still can't admit it. But I found the best part of myself when I found you.

I remember that when I met you—the first time we spoke at each other when you heckled me at the comedy club in Tampa and the first time we met face-to-face in LA—despite all the cocky banter, I was afraid I didn't have enough to offer any woman as a partner. But it turns out I will always offer you whatever you need because you make me want to be the right man and partner for you. I will always have more to give you, and there's always so much I want from you. You always provide Sam and me with exactly what we need.

You're the setup and the story arc and the main character and the conflict and the punchline.

Our shopping carts runneth over.

We didn't show each other our vows as we were writing them in our joke notebooks, but I did just happen to see a page from one of your old joke notebooks when I was carrying a box of them into my house back when you were moving in with me. I think you know by now that you can always ask me anything, but there's a question you had a couple of years ago about something. I'm happy to answer it now...

The winking emoticon does mean I like like you.

So does the winking face emoji.

Every emoji and emoticon I use in a message to you, every word I write or say to you means that I like you, Frankie Hogan, very soon to be Frankie Hogan-Brodie.

Because I like you.

I really like you.

And I love you.

A lot.

As a very wise, very young man once said—you're the only one who makes me smile with my eyes and laugh with my whole face. You make me so happy I don't even care how weird I look when I laugh really hard.

You'll always be the headliner and the better half of this asshole comedy duo.

It has been my pleasure to watch you blossom as a comedian and as a writer.

It has been my passion to have you as my lover and my best friend.

It has been my delight to see you care for my son.

It will be my joy and terror to raise the baby who's growing inside of you.

It's my great honor to finally marry you.

And I'm going to be the funniest, best-looking, best and only fucking husband you ever have.

With this ring, I thee wed.

I'll never get over myself, and I will never, ever get over you.

If you loved Shane Miller, Nico Todd, Alex Vega, and Grammie Todd, you can find them in the Name in Lights series — SLEEPER, CHARMER, TROUBLEMAKER.

Listen to the amazing multicast duet audiobook! Narrated by Teddy Hamilton & Emma Wilder, featuring Zachary Webber, Jason Clarke, Mackenzie Cartwright, and Connor Crais

ABOUT THE AUTHOR

USA Today bestselling author Kayley Loring spent many years as a screenwriter (under a different name) in Los Angeles before moving to the Pacific Northwest to live out her childhood dream of being a Disney heroine who talks and sings to woodland creatures. When not trying to keep animals alive, she's writing steamy romantic comedy novels, obviously. She's breathing cleaner air, writing dirtier words, and staring at her computer screen until her eyeballs dry out instead of prancing around Southern California in miniskirts and going to the hair salon. Still waiting for the woodland creatures to clean her house, though.

Read or listen to Kayley's books when you want to laugh, warm your heart, and enjoy top-notch banter, strong heroines who need to be chased, lovable characters you'd want to know in real life, and swoon over perfectly imperfect book boyfriends.

www.kayleyloring.com

**You'll find tons of Brodies merch in
The Kayley Store!**
https://kayleyloring.com/product-category/
merchandise/

Made in the USA
Las Vegas, NV
24 October 2024